TOO CLOSE FOR COMFORT

Emily has shut herself away to work in the family's old holiday cottage in remotest West Cornwall. Her two Jack Russells are all the company she needs . . . until the night she rescues a stranger injured in a raging storm. Cut off by bad weather, and with no telephone, they have to sit it out. Emily begins to warm to Adam. But who is he — and why does he want to stay with her once the storm has passed?

CHRISSIE LOVEDAY

TOO CLOSE FOR COMFORT

Complete and Unabridged

LINFORD
Leicester

First published in Great Britain in 2007

First Linford Edition
published 2007

British Library CIP Data

Loveday, Chrissie
   Too close for comfort.—Large print ed.—
Linford romance library
   1. Love stories
   2. Large type books
   I. Title
   823.9′2 [F]

   ISBN 978–1–84617–908–2

Published by
F. A. Thorpe (Publishing)
Anstey, Leicestershire

Set by Words & Graphics Ltd.
Anstey, Leicestershire
Printed and bound in Great Britain by
T. J. International Ltd., Padstow, Cornwall

This book is printed on acid-free paper

1

The rain was hammering down. He struggled to keep his footing on the steep path. It was like trying to climb a waterfall. He gritted his teeth and toiled on. Darkness had come early with the storm and he was still a long way from his intended target. He tripped over a rock and plunged down the side of the path, rolling over and over until he hit against boulder and lay very still.

★ ★ ★

Emily stirred the logs on the fire and made a blaze. She huddled closer to the fire and the two Jack Russells pushed past her to get their share of the warmth.

'Hey you rotten pair, I need warming too.' Their ears pricked up as she spoke and they looked hopefully towards the door.

'Oh no. You can forget any ideas of walks. We're in for the night.'

The little cottage looked cosy and inviting. Emily smiled as memories flooded back. She had known this place since she was a small child. It was the scene of childhood holidays since her parents had inherited the place many, many years ago.

The remote spot in West Cornwall seemed far away from the rest of the world and was the perfect place to shut herself away and finish her work. She was trying to complete her latest assignment, the illustrations for a high profile children's book that was certain to be in the Christmas stockings of most children the following year. She had been thrilled to get the commission and had completed over half the drawings.

She had come to Cornwall to seek inspiration, as well as finding a bit more time to work without the interruptions of normal life in her flat in Hertford-shire.

Besides, it was a good excuse to have some space for the dogs. They loved racing along the beaches and over the moors, obviously believing they were in doggy heaven. In theory, this was all fine, until the February weather had hit.

There had been storms for several nights and everywhere was soaked. There were rivulets running down into every valley and the lane leading to the cottage was totally waterlogged. But Emily wasn't worried. She had a good supply of tinned food and if she was stuck at home for several days, she could see no problems.

Her contemplation in front of the fire came to a sudden end as the lights went out.

'Drat,' she cursed as she rose and looked for some candles. They usually kept a stock under the kitchen sink and she groped around to find them. Matches were the next problem, but she managed to strike one and lit her candle. 'OK dogs. Looks like we have a problem here.' She thought the power would come on again in a short time and if it didn't, she always had her mobile phone she could use to call the power provider.

'Maybe I should get a few more logs in,' she muttered to the dogs. Tails wagging, they accompanied her to the door and dashed out into the night once it was open. They charged around barking, excited by the wind and the strange noises. They ran to the gate and began barking persistently.

'Come in you silly dogs,' shouted Emily, her voice blown back at her by the ferocious wind. But they continued barking. 'What is it?' she shouted, crossing towards the creaking gate. 'What can you hear?' she added uncertainly. Amidst the howling of the air rushing through trees and the rattle of chimes, she wondered if maybe, she had heard a faint cry.

The dogs were silent for a moment and then began their barking again. She went back inside and picked up her coat and scarf. She pulled on some boots and found an old torch.

'This is total madness,' she told the dogs as they ran ahead towards the sound she thought she might have heard.

Sliding along the treacherous path, a route she knew like the back of her hand in daylight, she continued towards the steep dip that led into the valley. One way led eventually to the coast, about three miles away and the other path led high on to the moor.

She took the moorland side and shone the faint torch beam ahead of her, praying that she didn't slide back down the steep slope. The dogs rushed away from her, diving beneath the battered gorse bushes and once more, beginning their frantic barking.

'Snickett . . . Susie,' she shouted, her voice faint against the wind. 'Have you found something?' She sighed. 'I bet you've only found a rabbit who's daft enough to be out on a night like this.'

The rain began lashing down once more and she tugged the hood over her already soaking hair. 'Come on, dogs,' she called crossly. 'I knew I was mad to listen to you.' But the little dogs didn't return to her. They barked on and on and she peered down the ridge.

She shone the feeble torch beam down to see if anything showed. Was there a faint glimpse of yellow? She moved the torch again. There was indeed something, right next to where the dogs were standing.

'Hello? Is somebody down there?' she called. There was a faint wail.

'Help me. Please help me.' It was a male voice.

'It's OK. I'm on my way.'

As Emily clambered down the slope, she lost her footing and slid on her bottom, following the route made by the fallen man. She landed in a heap beside him.

'Sorry. Hope I didn't land on top of you.'

'I'm just so relieved to see someone.

Even if you'd flattened me, I'd have been delighted. I'm afraid I've broken something. Ankle, leg, I don't know. It all just hurts like crazy.'

From what she could see, he was quite a large man and there was no way she was going to be able to lift him clear of the gully in which he'd landed. It was made especially difficult with the rain teeming down and making everywhere so slippery. She shone the torch over him. 'Do you have a pack of some sort?' she asked.

'I did have. I've slipped down here for quite some distance so I'm not sure when I became parted from it. But if you can find it, there's a mobile phone inside. Unless of course, you've got one with you.'

Emily cursed. She'd only left the house intending to see why the dogs were barking and hadn't thought to pick it up.

'No. I only went out to stock up wood for the fire. I wasn't really intending to come out on a rescue

7

mission. But it's much too dangerous to go looking around for anything. We have to try and work out how we're going to help you. There's no way I'm going to be able to lift you back up that slope.'

'Maybe we could find something I can haul myself along. A rope or a long branch. A ladder would be ideal, but . . .'

'But hardly practical. Even if I had one, I'd never get it here. But a rope sounds good. I'm sure there's at least one of those at the cottage.'

'You mean you live near here? Thank heavens.'

'Well, not far away. But it's not exactly a main highway between there and here. I'm Emily Tranter, by the way.'

'Adam Bryant. Look, I'm grateful to you coming out on such a foul night. But I do need to move very soon. I'm not sure how much damage I've done. Can you call someone?'

'I'll try, but the power's off at home.

I've only got a mobile phone and that doesn't get much of a reception in the cottage. I really think the priority is to try and move you from that hole. I'll go right back now and get a rope and try the phone.'

She scrambled back up the bank, praying that she could find some way of hauling a large man up a slippery mud bank with water cascading over them both. As she trotted carefully back, her mind was racing. She needed some sort of pulley.

Her brother had used one when he was messing about with car engines and he could lift huge weights on his own with the aid of something like that. All Simon's old climbing ropes must be stored somewhere. They'd be ideal if she could sort them out quickly enough. She'd just have to wind the rope round a tree or something and hope that Adam whatever his name was, would be able to help himself.

*   *   *

9

The cottage was still in darkness. The faint glimmer of the candle could be seen through the sitting room window. Emily rushed inside, trying to remember where the ropes were stored. She knew she'd seen some recently. Her brother, Simon, used to go rock climbing and he'd always left everything here at the cottage.

She burrowed into the cupboard under the stairs and dragged out a box. Bingo, she muttered as she held the candle nearer. There were various clips with loops of rope attached as well as a long length of good quality rope. It all looked most useful. She looped the coil over her shoulders and stuffed the rest of the bits and pieces into a rucksack. She picked up her mobile phone but as she'd expected there was no signal.

She felt more confident as she made the journey back to Adam, She was already more familiar with the track and even managed to save the torch batteries for where they were most needed.

'Hi. You OK?' she called when she was near the place.

'Never better,' he called back with heavy sarcasm. 'Sorry. I'm very grateful to you. Any luck with the phone?'

'Sorry, no. But I've got plenty of ropes and stuff. OK. I'm coming down in a mo.' She left the stick on the path and unpacked the rope loops and clips. If she could secure them round his body, he could then use his hands to help heave himself up.

Meanwhile, she needed to find a stout tree to loop the rope around. There was nothing. All the trees were thin and mere saplings and wouldn't be nearly strong enough to carry his weight. Maybe there was a boulder that would do. In the dark, it was difficult to move around, but finally she found something that she thought would do the trick.

'Right. I'm coming down now. I've got a sort of harness you can use. Save your strength a bit.' It was a much easier descent using the rope as a sort of hand rail and she was soon standing beside him, feeling triumphant. 'OK. You need to hook this under your arms, around your middle and then clip this thing on to the rope. I'll make another knot to hold it.'

'You seem to know all about this. Do you make a habit of rescuing injured men from mountain paths?' He forced his tone to be light, but he was gritting his teeth as pain shot up his leg when he tried even the smallest movement.

'That was a bad one, wasn't it?' Emily asked sympathetically. 'Maybe we should try something else. Try to put some sort of tent over you until daylight and try to get help.'

'I'll give this a shot first. It's OK. I'd just been in one position for too long. What's the next stage?'

'I'll go to the top again and try to haul you up. You'll have to help of course, but you should be able to heave on your arms and save the leg.'

'I'm a bit of a weight for a girl to manage.'

'I've made a sort of pulley out of another rope. We'll manage.' She climbed back and began to tighten the rope. 'You ready?' she called.

'You're amazing. Go for it. OK. Steady . . . yes. I'm moving.'

The two Jack Russells were rushing up and down the slope, still barking. Emily yelled at them to keep out of the way. She heaved on the rope and felt the weight dragging as she pulled. There was a sudden flash of lightning, followed by a roll of thunder. That's all I need, thought Emily. She heaved again and felt some movement.

'On . . . my . . . way . . . up,' Adam called grimly. His face was twisted with pain, but the adrenaline was kicking in and giving him added strength. He knew he had to reach the top if he was going to survive. At last, he arrived on the path and lay in a heap, panting, 'Well done, Emily. You're a miracle worker.'

She sat down heavily beside him, her own breath coming in gasps.

'First stage over with. Just have to

drag you back to the cottage now. If possible, the rain's heavier than ever. Now, there's a walking stick somewhere around here. I think you may have landed on top of it. That will be a bit of help. With me on one side and the walking stick on the other, we should manage fine.'

'Are you always this optimistic? And well equipped?'

'I try. Now, have you got your breath back? We have to get you to your feet somehow. Unhook the ropes and leave them there. I can always come back for them later, preferably in daylight, tomorrow morning.'

They managed to heave him to his feet and leaning heavily on the stick and with an arm around Emily's shoulders, they began to move along the path. They had to stop every few yards as pain surged through the man's body. But he was fit and strong and soon started to move again. After what felt like an eternity, the cottage came into view.

'Not much further,' Emily panted, relieved for herself as much as for him. The dogs had run ahead, seeing home territory and were already waiting by the door. 'OK. I'll get a chair for you,' she said as they went into the tiny room. 'And I'll get more candles.'

Adam collapsed on to the chair and sat still. Emily busied herself putting more wood on the fire and filled a kettle. Luckily, the cottage had a tank of gas outside, for the cooker, so she was able to make hot drinks for them both.

'We'd better get you out of these wet things.' She unzipped his jacket and peeled it off. It had kept him fairly dry underneath, but he was still rather too damp to leave his clothes on. 'I'm not sure if it's your leg or ankle that's broken. If it is broken at all. You need the wet things to be removed, but without damaging anything. I'm sorry, but I think we have to cut the waterproofs to get them off.'

'They cost me a fortune,' he groaned.

'But, you're right. I have to remove them.'

'And the boots. You'll get gangrene if we leave your feet soaking wet.'

'Have you got shares in the outdoor clothing market?' Adam tried to joke. 'Do whatever you have to.'

Quickly, she sliced through the laces and peeled away the soaking leather of his expensive boots. The injured foot was very swollen and she toyed with the idea of leaving the boot for support. But with wet socks, the circulation would be too restricted and he could surely suffer even more damage.

Apologising again, she steadily cut through the stitching until the boot was lying almost flat. With sharp scissors, she cut away his sock and looked at the damaged ankle.

'You know, I think it might just be a very bad sprain. Can't tell much without an X-ray of course and it's very bruised and swollen. No signs of any bones protruding.' She fetched a towel and wrapped it gently round the foot.

16

'Glad to hear it,' he grimaced. 'You clearly know something about first aid?' Adam suggested.

She shook her head.

'Not really.'

'Anyway, you seem to know what you're doing. Thank you again. Get off,' he added as two very wet dogs tried to climb on his knee.

'Snickett. Sue. Get down. Come here.' She rubbed them with a towel and they went to lie in front of the fire, eyes never leaving this strange man whom their mistress had brought home.

'You should get yourself out of your wet things,' Adam suggested. 'I need you to stay healthy.' His dark brown eyes crinkled at the corner and he managed a swift smile before another wave of pain hit him.

She was beginning to shiver, despite rushing around and knew she must get out of her own wet things. But Adam would be suffering from shock any time now and he'd begin to feel very cold. She looked in Simon's cupboard.

Great. There were several sweaters and T-shirts in there as well as some jog pants.

Once she'd drunk some hot tea, things began to look better. Adam got dressed in her brother's sweater and had a little more colour in his face. He was rather good looking, she decided. Mid brown hair, slightly curling and the most gorgeous dark brown eyes. He gave her a brave smile.

'Thanks so much,' he said again. 'I really began to wonder if anyone was going to find me before it was too late. What time is it? My watch has stopped.'

'About ten o'clock. Look, if we're going to get any help here, I shall have to try and get up the track to the road. There may be some reception there. For some reason, it varies and one day I can get a signal and the next, the mobile's just dead. Will you be all right for a little while?'

'Course. But take care. It's still pouring down and your outdoor things are all wet.'

'Don't worry. I'm sure there are some more waterproofs somewhere. We tend to leave them here after holidays.'

'I see. So this isn't your home? And who's the 'we' you mention?'

'I'll tell you all about it later. I want to try for help right now. OK. I'll leave the dogs here to keep you company.'

'No, really. Take them . . . ' His voice faded as she went out of the door. The dogs howled, not wanting to be left behind. 'OK, you guys,' he said to the two dogs. 'I don't much like dogs, understand? You stay by the fire and I won't bother you.' They sat down and wagged their tails just a little at the sound of his voice. One of them leaned her nose on his uninjured foot and sighed. He eyed her suspiciously, but called a truce.

Outside, Emily ploughed her way up the long track that led to the cottage. It was almost half a mile to the main road and any hope of making her phone call.

The rain continued to pour out of black skies and she wondered if the little bridge at the end of the track would still be holding. There was a stream that ran down from the moors and went along the side of the road for several miles, eventually heading off towards the sea. Just before the end of the track, there was an old wooden bridge which had to be crossed to reach the road.

The track became more and more waterlogged and some distance from the road, her feet were in running water. The stream had obviously burst its banks and the ground was flooded. She was at least a hundred yards from the bridge. Even if it had survived the torrent, she wasn't going to be able to go much further.

2

She held her phone up high and peered
to see if she could get any signal.
Emergency service only it said on the
screen. Thank heavens, she breathed.
Exactly what she needed. She pressed
the keys and waited. There was a
crackling sound and she could barely
make out a voice.

'This is Emily calling from Tranter's
Cottage, Penullian. I have an injured
man at the cottage. We're cut off. No
electricity and the track's flooded.
Please send help.' She had no idea
whether her message had been heard by
anyone. The crackling persisted and she
repeated the message, praying that
someone could make out what she was
saying. The phone went dead. One
short bleep told her the battery was
low, just before it all shut down.

She'd been meaning to put it on to

charge all day and had forgotten. Too late now, she realised and turned back to the cottage. She felt frozen through and wetter than she could ever remember. Wearily, she toiled her way back to the cottage and pushed the door open.

'Gosh, I'm freezing,' she moaned and slipped out of the wet jacket. She went to the fire and held out her hands to the warmth.

'Any luck?' asked Adam. 'Did you manage to get through to anyone?'

'I don't know. I spoke to a load of crackles and I don't know if anyone could make out what I was saying. Then the battery went dead.'

'You're kidding? How could someone as efficient as you allow a battery to get low?'

'I hadn't expected the power to go off and nor did I expect to be attempting to drown myself in a storm. I shall go and change yet again and then I'll make another hot drink.'

'I'm sorry, Emily. Really I am. I'm

just so frustrated.'

'OK. I know.'

Once she was warmer and dry again, she began to feel better. She warmed some soup from one of the cans in her store cupboard and began to relax a little. She knew in her heart that her message wouldn't bring any help, not tonight. She needed to make some sort of plans for Adam. There was no way he would get upstairs to a bed so she would have to organise something down here. She also needed to try and reduce the swelling on his ankle.

'I think there are some frozen peas in the freezer compartment.'

'The soup was fine, thanks,' he said with a feeble grin. She ignored him.

'I'll put them on your ankle to see if we can make that swelling go down a bit. It might help us to see what's going on. Even though the power's been off for some time, the peas should still be frozen.'

She wrapped the bag of peas in a damp towel and put it carefully over the swelling. He complained bitterly, but accepted it might do some good. She then set about organising blankets and pillows on the sofa. She looked doubtfully at the length of him.

It was well after midnight before she was able to get into her own bed. For once, she allowed her dogs to sleep on the bed beside her. She needed their warmth and they were delighted to cuddle close to their beloved mistress. Exhausted, she fell into a deep sleep.

Adam was less fortunate. He could not get comfortable and was in severe pain. At least he was warm and dry, he tried to convince himself. As soon as it was light, his saviour would be able to find his own mobile telephone and summon help. Maybe her own message had got through and someone was on the way right now.

As the hours slowly passed, he knew it was less and less likely. He tugged the blankets around himself. The fire had almost burnt out and the room had grown colder. The candles were also practically gone. He slipped into a shallow sleep and waited for something to happen.

Emily awoke with a start and looked at the bedside clock. Five-thirty. The memory of the previous evening rushed back and she leapt out of bed. The fire would be out and Adam would be cold. The dogs complained at having their sleep disturbed and curled up into their warm place again. She piled on several layers of clothes and went down the stairs.

'Hi,' Adam said. 'I'm so glad to see you.'

'Did you manage to sleep at all?' Emily busied herself putting logs on the ashes and fanned it slightly, hoping to set them alight.

'I guess I dozed a bit. Doesn't look as though your message was received. Unless they've been flying round in circles all night looking for us.'

'How about some breakfast? I'll need to use up some of the perishable stuff pretty quickly if the power stays off. I can offer bacon and eggs. Maybe a sausage. Probably all sorts of odd things.'

They chatted over a large breakfast and she discovered that he was taking an early holiday, hiking though the wilder parts of Cornwall before the season started.

'I'm planning a trip to South America later in the year. Thought this might be a good preparation.'

'Sounds ambitious, but I'd hardly consider dear old Cornwall as preparation for that. You'll need a new pair of boots,' she added ruefully.

She told him about her own life and work. He wanted to see her drawings. Shyly, she produced her portfolio.

'Wow. These are extremely beautiful. Amazing detail. You are so talented. But why come here to work? You've hardly got all the mod cons, have you?'

'I love this place. I wanted the inspiration of the area. It's still largely unspoilt and well, I can be right away from distractions. Or so I thought.' She grinned and nodded towards him.

'Oh, so I'm a distraction am I?'

'Could be. I'm not exactly working right now, am I?' She glanced through the window at the faint dawn light. 'At least the rain's eased off. The wind seems to have dropped too.'

'Maybe you can go and look for my mobile? Then we can call for help and I can get out of this place.' She frowned at his rather rude words.

'Assuming the battery is still OK and the phone's not damaged.'

'Sorry. I'm not a good patient. I'm usually the one in control and not good at taking orders or being helpless.'

'So I gather. I'll go out when it's properly light. No more risks. At least you're warm and dry and now, well fed. I still don't know how you came to be in such a lonely place so late?'

'I was supposed to be getting to St Just last night. But the rain came in and it got dark very much earlier than I was expecting. I'd been lying down my hole for a couple of hours before you found me.'

'You were hopeful to start with. It's at least four or five miles to St Just. Maybe more. You won't be able to make any such errors in South America.'

'Maybe I'd better take you along with me. You seem like the sort of person who would keep me safe.' She stared at him but made no comment.

'I'll clear up the breakfast stuff and then I'll go and see if I can find your belongings. And rescue the ropes and stuff. Simon would be furious if it all got ruined or lost.'

'I have to say, it's not every day someone can be rescued from the jaws of death by a beautiful young woman. Won't you tell me about yourself, Emily Tranter?'

'You're obviously feeling better. But now, I'm going to recover the gear. Maybe we can talk when I get back.' She pulled on her boots, still soggy from the previous night and found a dry anorak. The dogs bounded to the door, tails wagging furiously at the thought of an outing. She waved goodbye and left her patient wrapped in blankets, his injured foot propped high on a cushion.

The track was thoroughly soaked and even more slippery than the previous night. She wondered how on earth they had managed to negotiate such a narrow path without further disaster. She came to the place where the ropes had been left and eased herself down the incline to where Adam had fallen.

She looked around for his back pack and spotted something deep in the gully. It looked pretty much irretrievable but she went towards it, spurred on by the thought of a mobile phone that would work. They needed outside help and this looked like the only way to get it quickly.

Praying that she didn't fall herself, she fastened the rope round her middle and used it to lower herself towards the bright yellow pack.

When she finally reached it, she opened it and searched for the precious phone. It was there, but with a great crack across the glass screen. It was dead as a dodo.

She hoisted the pack to her shoulders and began the long climb back. Without the ropes, she could never have made it and she sat panting when she finally reached the top.

At least Adam would be reunited with his belongings, but apart from that, Emily felt she had wasted an awful lot of energy for no useful purpose. She untied the ropes and coiled them around her shoulder and set off back home. The dogs had rushed up and down the steep slopes without hesitation.

'It's all right for you, you've got four legs each,' she told them. 'And you don't have a ton of wet rope to carry.'

By the time she returned, she felt totally exhausted. Adam was dozing and opened his eyes at the noise of their return.

'Any luck?' he asked.

'I got everything, but your phone's had it. I checked. I'm afraid we're stuck here until the water goes down. How's the ankle feeling now?'

'Pretty sore. I'm feeling sort of stiff all over but maybe that's the result of the fall and not moving around much. Look, maybe the battery will fit your phone. Worth a try.'

'I'm afraid not. It's a totally different model. Mine is very basic, not one of these flashy modern things like yours.'

'Flashy or not. It's useless if it's broken.' He sighed and lay back, feeling cross and even more frustrated.

★　★　★

They talked for much of the day and gradually began to learn about each other. She discovered that Adam was thirty, three years older than her. He'd had several girlfriends, but claimed that he had always been too busy sorting out

31

his career to form a serious relationship with anyone.

He was actually rather vague about his job, saying that he worked for a large group of retail stores on the technical side. His home was a flat in the Midlands somewhere. He seemed intrigued by her work and spent a long time pouring over her detailed drawings for the book.

'These are just delightful,' he told her. 'You're very talented.' He looked thoughtful. 'Do you do other stuff? Besides book illustrations?'

'Depends what job I get. Yes, I can do other stuff. What are you thinking about?'

'Just an idea. I'll give it some more thought. If I can put some work your way, I'd feel it was a way of saying thank you for all of this.'

Emily felt comfortable in his presence. He was an easy person to like, despite his constant irritation with his plight. He was simply not used to spending time sitting still, certainly not without his various home comforts.

'I can't believe you don't have a phone here. And when do you think the power will be put back on? It's crazy.'

'Dad likes to get away from everything and doesn't want to be bothered by calls. Besides, we all have mobiles these days.'

'They even work sometimes, as long as you remember to re-charge the batteries.'

'All right. I know I was stupid, but I could hardly be expected to know all this was going to happen. Some idiot walking alone on the moors in the middle of a huge storm.'

'I didn't know there was going to be a storm.'

'Exactly. You should have listened to a weather forecast. Oh come on. We shouldn't bicker. We don't know each other well enough,' she added with a grin.

'Sorry. I just feel so darned helpless. I hate having to be so reliant on someone else. And thanks again.' He held out a hand and took hers. It felt good. He had strong fingers, no doubt from spending his days tapping away at some computer.

'I ought to put some more ice on the swelling. Haven't got any more though. The freezer is only a tiny compartment in the fridge and with the power off . . . That reminds me. I ought to cook some of the stuff in there before it goes off. Can you manage some pasta?'

'Sounds great. I'd offer to open a bottle of wine, under other circumstances.'

'I'm going out for another look down the track before I start. It hasn't rained for a bit and the water may have gone down. If I can get through I can maybe get help. Nobody really knows I'm here and they certainly won't realise the power is off.'

'Don't your parents know where you are?'

'I said I was coming down here, but I doubt they took it in. They're so busy with their own lives since Dad retired.

Always going here and there. I phone them every now and again, but that's about it, till Mum decides we need a family get together. But what about you? Won't someone be missing you?'

'I suppose the hotel will wonder where I've gone. My car's still parked there. You know, maybe you've got something there. They might mount a search for me.'

'Did you tell them where you were going?'

'Actually, no. Nobody knows where I am. Nice idea while it lasted. I took a bus from Penzance and planned to walk over the moor and then catch a bus back.'

'I'd better go and see what's happening.' She got up and once more, put on boots and coat and went out into another storm. She ploughed her way along the track towards the road, but the water was swirling around faster than ever. There was no way she could wade through it. She couldn't even see the road so there was no point in leaving any sort of help sign, an idea she'd thought of earlier.

They just had to sit it out until someone realised they needed help. How long was it safe to leave Adam without proper medical attention? Would the logs for the fire last out? Would the gas last until she could get out to order more? Suddenly, she felt as helpless as Adam. What a ridiculous situation. Feeling near to tears herself, she turned and went back to the cottage.

3

'Your dogs are a bit pushy, aren't they?' Adam greeted her when she returned. 'Look at them.'

She smiled. Both Jack Russells were curled on the sofa beside Adam. One sat with her head tucked into his arm and the other was stretched out along his legs. She laughed.

'Typical. They do like their comfort. Look, I'm afraid we're still trapped. The water's risen, if anything. I guess it's still coming down from the moor and will be some time before it's going to drop.'

Adam grimaced. 'Great. I just hope you're right about this being a sprain and that I'm not doing untold damage that will involve operations and endless treatment to put it right.'

'Cheer up. We're warm and dry. There's food and the means of cooking it.' Emily crossed her fingers as she spoke, hoping all her earlier thoughts of doom and gloom were just thoughts and not premonitions. 'Now, pasta and some sort of sauce. I'll see what I can find. I think there's some mince needs using and some mushrooms and other stuff.' She busied herself as Adam watched. She turned on the television, thinking it might keep him occupied for a while.

'Needs electricity,' he remarked wryly. 'As does your music system and doubtless the radio.'

'Yes. Actually, we may have batteries for the radio. At least we can hear the news.'

'Don't know that I want to,' he replied gloomily.

'Oh for heavens sake. I know this is an unpleasant situation, but please stop moaning. I'd much rather be getting on with my work with adequate lights and everything. I'm going to open some wine and you can see if that cheers you up.'

'Come here,' he commanded. 'Sit near me.' She obeyed him, wondering what was coming next. He took her hand and pulled her fingers to his lips. He kissed them gently and smiled at her. She felt her heart beating quite extraordinarily hard. 'I'm so sorry. You are an absolute angel and I'm really only moaning at the world, not you. Forgive me?'

Emily stared into the darkest brown eyes she could ever remember seeing. She felt her irritation sweeping away and began to think she was indeed fortunate to have him with her. Being alone in this situation might seem more than a little scary. She smiled.

''Course I forgive you. I do understand and I was also only blowing my top a bit.'

'There's something else I have to say. I know this is also probably a sort of heresy to you, but I don't much like dogs. That's why I was a bit off about them lying on me.'

'Snickett. Sue, get down immediately.

I'm sorry. I didn't realise. Come off you two.' The dogs stared at her with very hurt expressions. Very slowly, they lifted themselves, stretched and slid off the sofa. They both shook and then sat down staring at her. 'You're a spoilt pair of brats,' she told them as her mouth quivered with a grin.

'Actually, what I should have said is that I never used to like dogs. I can feel a cold patch where they were sitting. These two seem quite nice really. For dogs.'

Emily laughed.

'Love me, love my dogs, eh? Now, if you let go of my hand, I'll see about some supper.'

'If you must. I quite like holding it actually.' She found herself blushing and pulled away. However helpless he may feel at this moment, she was aware that he was a most attractive man and probably he knew it. She felt self conscious as she put together the simple meal under his watchful gaze. The contents of the fridge were now far from cold and needed using up.

If they did eat everything however, they had no idea of how long they might be stormbound. She stirred everything into the sauce. It would be a pity to waste it.

The sitting-room in the little cottage looked particularly welcoming in the candlelight. Romantic, almost. She tried to think of this as any other evening she might have entertained a friend for supper. When the meal was over, wondering how to entertain him, she brought out the Scrabble game. He frowned and informed her in a superior sounding tone that he didn't play board games.

'Then it's high time you started,' she said decisively. 'In the absence of other forms of entertainment, you can learn.' She dealt out the tiles and told him the rules.

'I know how to play. I just don't like playing.'

She ignored him and continued to sort out her letters.

'Come on,' she ordered. 'I refuse to sit here listening to you moaning all evening.' As she spoke there was a sudden click and the lights came on.

'Hallelujah!' he called out. 'Quick, plug your phone in and call for help.'

'Don't be silly. The battery will take hours to charge. It's flat out.'

'But you can use it with the mains plugged in. Come on. Quickly.'

She looked uncertainly at him but it was worth a try. Besides, one never knew if the power was restored permanently or if this was just a trial run. She sorted the plugs and pressed the buttons.

'It's working. Hello? Yes. I'm calling from Tranter's Cottage, Penullian. Yes. Out on the St Just road. I have an injured man here. He may have a broken ankle. We need an ambulance, but the track leading to the cottage is flooded. I think the stream's burst its banks. The power's been off for ages and only just come back . . . ' There was a sudden bang and the lights went out again and the phone was dead once more.

'Damn, damn, damn,' Adam cried out. 'Do you think they have enough information to send someone?'

'I hope so. The operator seemed to take in where I meant, and she'll have the number of the call recorded.'

Scrabble forgotten, they both became restless, waiting for something to happen. They speculated about the power and why it had only come on for so short a time.

'They probably thought it was fixed, but something was still shorting out. I somehow doubt we'll get help tonight. I didn't manage to get enough information to them about your injuries. They probably won't treat it as a huge priority. All the same, I'll sleep on the armchair, just in case anyone comes.'

'You need to rest,' he protested. 'I'll call out if I hear anything.'

They finished the game, which despite his comments, he had seemed to enjoy. She put more logs on the fire and hoped it would last till morning. Later, she settled down on the chair and the dogs climbed up beside her. Adam was made as comfortable as possible for the night. With the power still off, she left just one candle alight in case they needed it quickly. It was not easy to fall asleep and she wriggled to get more comfortable. The dogs, cross at being disturbed, left her and climbed on the sofa with Adam.

'Hello you two. Come to keep me warm?'

'Is that OK? Do you want me to call them off?'

'It's all right. They are quite comforting actually. For dogs,' he added.

They were silent for a while, both trying to sleep.

'You still awake?' he whispered softly. Emily grunted.

'I am now.'

'Sorry. Only if you are awake, I'm really thirsty. Any chance of some water?'

She sighed and hauled herself up.

'Do you want a hot drink? There's only milk powder left. The fresh milk has all gone.'

'Water's fine. Sorry.'

She gave him a drink and went to look out of the window. It was pitch black outside. Her assumption that nobody would be here till morning, looked accurate. She gave a sigh, partly of frustration, partly anxious about her impatient patient.

'I'll have one more shot at sleeping then I might try to do some work,' she muttered.

'You'll strain your eyes,' Adam told her.

They settled down and both fell into a sort of doze. It must have been about six o'clock when the dogs began to growl. They leapt off the sofa and began to bark, fully arousing both of them. Emily went to the window and saw lights flashing outside.

'Hey, looks as if we're being rescued. There's someone out there.' She went to the door and the dogs rushed out.

'Hello?' she called.

'Is this Tranter's Cottage?' shouted a male voice.

'It is. Thanks so much for coming.'

'You phoned the emergency services? Someone had an accident? Haven't you got any lights?'

'We've got candles, but no power. It just came on for a few minutes, but then went off again. I just about managed a phone call.'

Two men clad in yellow oilskins came into the cottage. They seemed to fill the place. Adam sat up and grinned.

'Oh boy, am I glad to see you. Have you got an ambulance somewhere near?'

'Afraid not. We're police. The call got patched through to us and we came to see what was the problem. We've had to wade through a positive torrent. The track's still blocked. We'd have to get the helicopter in, but that's tricky because of this site. Rather too many trees. Maybe we should call a para-medic to assess the situation,' the

46

spokesman said to his colleague.

'We don't think his leg's broken but of course, without an X-ray, we can't be sure. He can wriggle his toes,' Emily told them.

'Sounds hopeful.'

'Do you mind not talking about me as if I'm not here,' Adam protested. 'I can speak for myself.'

'Sorry, sir. I'll radio back and see what we can do. Probably not much, till it's properly light. How long is it since the accident?'

'Days,' he moaned.

'About thirty-six hours. It was late, the day before yesterday,' Emily corrected.

'Seems much longer. I feel as if I've been lying on this wretched sofa for weeks.'

'Not the easiest of patients, I can see. Are you Adam Bryant, by any chance? Staying at the Bay Hotel, Penzance?'

'Yes, that's right. But . . . '

'The manager called us. You didn't return after a walking trip. I must say,

I'm glad we don't have to initiate a full-scale search over the moors. There are hundreds of gullies and places where someone could be hidden for days.'

The policemen went outside to use their radio and presumably, to organise the rescue.

'Well, looks like it's all over. I can't thank you enough for all you've done, and I'm sorry for being such a grump. I'll be in touch of course, to let you know what happens.'

'Hang on. I'm not letting you go off into the wild blue yonder. You're in no state to drive yourself anywhere, and they probably won't keep you in hospital, even if something's broken. You might need me again.'

'I couldn't impose. Thanks though. Really, I'll be fine.'

It was some hours before he could finally get to the hospital. Once it was properly light, everything began to move. The first blessing was that the power was restored. Whether it was coincidence or because the police had called, Emily did not know. But she was most relieved and immediately began to charge the battery in her phone and made tea for everyone.

'At least you can call me and let me know how you are,' she told Adam. 'I'm desperate for a shower . . . do you mind if I have one quickly? Won't be long.'

When she came down again, there was activity outside. A paramedic arrived to assess the situation and somehow later on, Adam was lifted over the water and put into the ambulance. Emily watched from the other side of the torrent and waved as the doors were finally shut. She could now get back to her ordinary life and begin working again.

All the same, as she walked back to the cottage, she felt strangely bereft. She went back inside and began to clean and tidy. She shook out the blankets, deciding they needed a wash once the weather improved. She cleaned out the fridge and switched it back on, though clearly she needed supplies to put into it. There were still plenty of tinned goods so it wasn't too urgent.

'I suppose there's no excuse not to get on with some work,' she said aloud. The dogs responded with wagging tails and hopeful expressions. 'OK. You win. Just a short walk.'

Everywhere smelt fresh and clean after so much rain. Though it had stopped and the wind was blowing and drying everything, it was still treacherous along the track and she walked cautiously, not wishing to share the fate of her recent guest.

The gorse was coming into flower. Brilliant gold shoots were sprouting from winter dark prickles, and under shaded spots, she found several clumps of primroses in bloom. The dogs tore around, loving the freedom after a couple of days of being kept inside.

She went to the end of the track. Miraculously, the wooden bridge had already reappeared as the flow of water was slowing down. She tested it and decided it was almost passable again. With great care, in another hour or two, she would be willing to risk driving over it to collect some groceries.

'Come on, pups,' Emily called, refreshed by the good, clear air.

After a cup of coffee, she spread out her drawing materials and settled down to work. It was almost midday when the phone rang.

'Emily?' Adam's voice said. 'I'm really sorry to bother you again, but I have a problem.'

She listened carefully and gave the only possible answer.

'Of course, you can come back here. It's the best solution. We'll need some supplies, but we'll be fine. Just let me think how we can organise it. Call me back in about ten minutes.'

She switched the phone off and frowned. Evidently, it was a bad sprain, complicated with a suspected, damaged ligament. The hospital had strapped the injury with a splint to support the leg and given him a pair of crutches. He couldn't drive and the hotel certainly wouldn't cope with an injured guest. Short of an ambulance taking him all the way back to his home in the Midlands, he was stuck. The phone rang again.

'If you can get a taxi here, you can collect my car and me and drive us both back. How's the flood water?' he asked.

'Going down rapidly. I'm really surprised it's dropped so much already. But I can use my car to drive over. No need for the expense of a taxi.'

'I've ordered one. It should be with you in about ten more minutes.'

'But . . . '

'It's all arranged. I'll pay for it, of course. You can collect me and we'll go to the hotel together and collect my stuff and the car. I'll pay the bill and then I'm finished. Free.'

She switched off the phone and reached for her coat and handbag. He'd certainly taken quite a bit for granted. Suppose she'd said he couldn't come back with her? But he'd known she would welcome him. She'd more or less said so but all the same, she had mixed feelings, as she thought more about it. Did she really want a houseguest for an indefinite time? Especially one who could be so bored and edgy as Adam. She simply had no idea of what she was letting herself in for.

4

Emily stuffed a pair of shoes into her bag and pulled on her wellies. She wasn't going to ruin her decent shoes walking down the soggy track and she doubted the taxi would be willing to drive along it.

'No dogs, you're staying here.' They looked deeply hurt and sat down near the fire, glaring at her. She couldn't help but smile. 'I'll take you out again later, but now I'm going shopping. You'd starve if I didn't.' They looked at her and wagged their tails slightly. She grabbed her keys and set off along the track. The earth smelt damp and there was even traces of wild garlic making an early showing this year.

She waded through the last few inches of water and stood by the roadside, awaiting the promised taxi. It was at least twenty minutes before it arrived and the driver was extremely grumpy at having to make such a long drive at one of his busy times.

'Could have fitted in any number of local runs, in the time this takes,' he grumbled.

'At least you're getting paid for this trip,' Emily said with a grin. 'And I'm very pleased to see you. I've been cut off for several days.'

'You one of them there Tranters?' he asked.

'Yes indeed. It was my grandfather's cottage originally.'

'So you're not one them incomers then?'

'Well, not really. Though my family have used the place for holidays mostly. They are thinking of selling up now my brother and I have left home. We don't come down for family holidays any more.'

'But you're here now. Makes all the difference. You're not one of the emmets. I'm pleased to meet you. I knew the old man when I was a lad.

Good old boy 'e was.' The rest of the journey passed pleasantly, as Emily was now accepted as an honorary resident rather than one of the emmets, the Cornish term for visitors, who invaded the driver's home territory.

When they arrived at the hotel where Adam had been staying, she practically emptied her purse to pay him. He would have to reimburse her, she decided. After all, she could have used her own car but he'd insisted on collecting his own vehicle. She went into reception and explained the situation.

'Ah yes, Mr Bryant did telephone to explain. Nasty business for him. Would you like to go to his room and pack for him? I understand the car keys have been left there as well as his things. There is also the matter of the bill, of course.'

'Oh dear. I don't think I can pay that for him. How much does he owe you?' The manager named a price that made her gasp slightly. Her credit card would be way over the top if she settled his account. 'I'm afraid he'll have to pay it himself. Suppose I go and collect him from the hospital and bring him back here? I'll just need the car keys and I'll do his luggage when we get back.'

'Certainly, madam. I'm afraid we had to leave his room untouched for the extra days. His luggage, you understand. I'm afraid we have to charge for the room, even though he wasn't actually in residence.'

'Of course. I'll be back soon.'

She was shown to his car and she gave a small gasp.

'I daren't drive this,' she muttered as she saw the very expensive-looking sports car. There was nothing for it but to get inside and start the engine. Her own battered relic was slow and comfortable, but this one scared her half to death. She put it in gear and slowly pressed the pedal.

Smoothly and almost silently, it moved forward. It was gorgeous and a slow smile spread across her face. If only her brother could see her now . . . he'd be positively green with envy.

The small hospital car park was full and she stopped outside the main door, leaving the car illegally parked and assumed Adam would be ready for her. He was waiting inside the reception area.

'Good girl,' he exclaimed and hauled himself to his feet, using the crutches supplied by the hospital. 'See? I'm quite mobile, really.'

Emily felt her heart leap. Though they had only been parted for a relatively short time, seeing his handsome features again reminded her that she needed to be very careful with this man.

'I'm not sure how you're going to get into this car of yours. It's very low and not exactly spacious. You might have been better in mine, even if it is an old wreck by comparison. I was terrified of scratching this monster. I've never driven anything so powerful.'

'I'll manage somehow. Thanks so

much for doing all this. Was there any problem at the hotel?'

'Only the small matter of a large bill.'

'Don't worry, I'll write you a cheque.'

'I'm afraid I couldn't pay it. We have to go back there and collect your stuff anyhow.'

He seemed slightly put out that she hadn't paid his bill and surprised that she'd thought it expensive. With great difficulty, he was settled in the passenger seat. Emily's nerves were even greater. With him watching closely, she put the powerful car into gear and drove out of the hospital grounds rather more slowly than either of them were comfortable with.

She explained the need to collect shopping and other emergency supplies to replenish what they had used, like candles. He grumbled that he was tired and needed to get some rest.

She smiled sweetly and suggested he could have a nap while she was doing all the chores.

After returning to the hotel and

packing his things, she made a quick dash around the supermarket and stacked everything into the rather small space left in the car.

'Not exactly designed for a family shop, is it?' she remarked.

'I'm not exactly used to doing a family shop. Can we go home now, please? Oh, hang on. You did buy some decent wine and things, didn't you?'

'Well, I bought a couple of bottles, but whether you consider them decent or not, I'm not sure.'

'There's just one more thing,' he said as she was about to drive home. She looked enquiringly at him. 'Could we stop somewhere and buy me a new phone? Is there a shop anywhere near?'

'Well,' she began doubtfully. 'There are several shops in town, but there's nowhere near to park. Will an electrical store do? There's a big one on the by-pass.'

'You can go in and get something for me, can't you?'

She was not happy about buying

something so expensive, but asked the sales assistant to bring several out to the car so he could choose for himself. He picked out an expensive model with features she couldn't begin to understand and he handed over his credit card.

'Not used to working from a car,' the assistant joked. 'But when it's a car like this one, I've no objection at all. Had it long?' he asked Emily, clearly mistaking them for a couple.

'Not long,' she replied with a smile.

Adam apologised once more for his short temper and they drove off home. She didn't like to mention that she was also out of pocket for the taxi journey and had spent far more than usual on shopping to feed them both. He was obviously unaware that some people had to manage on a very tight budget.

'I hope this car's going to make it through the flood water. It's much lower than mine, and with all your stuff in it, it must be even lower than usual.'

'Take it slowly. I'm sure it will

survive. Just don't drive off your little bridge. I don't fancy paddling with all this strapping on my leg. Especially with only crutches as aids.'

Also praying she didn't drive off the edge of the still submerged bridge, she splashed the car safely through the water and soon arrived at the door of the cottage. Two ecstatic dogs rushed out as soon as the door was opened and barked their welcome to the visitor.

'Whoa, you dogs. Give a poor invalid a chance. You bowl me over and then you'll never get your home to yourselves again.' He hobbled inside and collapsed on to the sofa once again. 'Feels like home already,' he muttered. 'Gosh, I feel exhausted.'

'I'd better unload the car before it gets dark,' Emily suggested. 'Then I'll get us something to eat. I'm starving. I never got round to eating much today.'

'I'm quite peckish. But I could do with some liquid. The painkillers are wearing off and they gave me some more to take.'

'Then what were you doing asking for wine? You can't take that with painkillers.'

'I was thinking of the next few days. I shall be ready for a drink after that.'

She busied herself bringing in the shopping and Adam's luggage. The dogs dashed in and out with her, barely stopping for a moment. They barked excitedly, delighted to see people again and aware of the promised changes in routine. Much more exciting than sitting quietly while Emily worked.

'Have you got an extension lead?' Adam asked once he was settled. 'Only I need to charge the new phone and also my laptop. Once I've got that going, I can use it for e-mails and contact my office. They must be wondering why I've been out of touch for so long.'

'I need to sort out a room for you. I suppose you will be able to manage the stairs with the aid of the crutches?'

'Oh yes. I should think so, but I'd like to get the phone sorted as soon as possible. It might take awhile to transfer the old number.'

'I can only do one thing at a time,' Emily snapped. 'The dogs need feeding too, so you'll just have to wait. I'm not your secretary. Or your slave,' she added for good measure.

'Oh Lord. I'm sorry. I'm being unbearable again, aren't I?' He looked so contrite that she was forced to giggle.

'You are a bit, but I'll forgive you this time. Just realise my limitations, please. This is only a modest home and obviously, much less grand a place than you're used to, but you're very welcome as long as you can remember that.'

He smiled at her and she felt her heart turn over again. His beautiful warm brown eyes could melt solid ice, she was quite certain of it. No wonder he was giving out orders. Any female who worked for him was probably half in love with him and would do anything for him, and here she was, living in the same house for at least several days. It could be a very dangerous situation, despite his incapacity.

'Sorry. I'll try to be less demanding and wait my turn for attention in your busy schedule.'

'Right. Well as long as that's clear. I'll plug your phone in over there and once that is charged, you can plug in the laptop. I'm then going to feed the dogs. Next, organise dinner and while it's cooking, I'll make up a bed for you.'

He said nothing and she busied herself with the tasks. He watched her every move, an unfathomable expression on his face. 'Do you want the television on?' she asked, embarrassed by his attention.

'If you like. Might be good to catch up on the world events. Seems like forever since I heard any news.'

'So, what's the office all about?' she asked after dinner. 'What do you do exactly?' He seemed slightly defensive about his work and said vaguely that he worked for a chain of department stores in the Midlands. His role was vaguely to do with computers, she gathered, but he would say little more about it. 'And I assume you are on holiday at the moment?' she continued to probe.

'Just taking a few days off really. I can work from here though, once I'm back on-line. Don't you have a computer?' he asked suddenly. 'I could maybe use that?'

'I have nothing at all to do with such things. I don't want to know about them and don't begin to understand them. I'm a totally pen and paper person myself.'

He laughed and began to tell her about the wonders of modern technology, but she put her fingers in her ears and told him he might as well try to teach the dogs.

'I'll convince you before I'm done,' he promised. 'It would be so useful to your business. You can contact people instantly. Sort out jobs. Contracts. Everything, and you can have a website to show off your work.'

'I've no idea what you're talking

about. I'm perfectly happy with my drawing, and old fashioned letters are wonderful. I love it when the postman arrives. There's nothing like opening an envelope and seeing that friends have written with their own hands. It's personal, knowing they were the last people to touch that particular piece of paper. You can keep your e-mails and e-cards and all that stuff you can't even touch.'

'One day Emily Tranter, I shall drag you screaming into the twenty-first century.'

'Lay a finger on me and my Jack Russells will bite you to pieces.' Both dogs leapt up at her words, as if they understood what was she saying. 'See, they are ready to attack.' They both laughed and settled down to watch a documentary on the television.

Soon after nine o'clock, they were both yawning. After two nights with very little sleep, weariness was catching up on them and they decided to have an early night.

'I must get on with some work tomorrow,' Emily told him. 'I'm already way behind schedule. Maybe you can catch up on your office work at the same time.'

The next morning was fine and sunny and Emily awoke early. She could hear a gentle snoring coming from the guest bedroom so she crept down the stairs as quietly as she could, intending to go for a walk with the dogs before Adam was awake and doubtless, would be demanding breakfast. There was still a chill in the air and she wrapped up warmly to go into the stiff breeze that was blowing. At least she should be able to hang out a few of the wet clothes that were still lurking around the cottage.

Excitedly, the dogs scampered around, enjoying the freedom after the days of bad weather and being kept in. They pounced on imaginary rabbits and chased each other under bushes. Emily breathed the fresh air and felt as if her lungs had been cleaned out.

After half an hour, she turned to go back to the cottage and felt eager to get on with her work. First though, she needed to organise breakfast and make sure her guest was sorted out with his temporary office.

Back inside, she lit the wood burner and put some coffee on the brew. The scent of it was soon drifting up the stairs and just as she had thought, Adam was soon moving around. He called down to her.

'Do you think you could help me? I'm a bit wary of coming down the stairs on my own. I think I can sort of sit down and slither down, but I can't manage the crutches.' With some giggling, they managed to get him down and using the crutches, he heaved himself to his feet again once they reached the bottom. 'There, I thought I managed that rather well, didn't you?'

'Very good. I'll soon have you walking the dogs and ready to climb mountains again, but you do have to be careful. I expect you're going to need some physiotherapy. Now, are you ready for some breakfast?'

'Great. I'm starving again. Must be the sea air. I'm never much for breakfast normally. Just some toast and that's it, but here, I seem to want the full English, as they say.'

'I'll get started then. I don't usually have much for lunch, so it's nice to start with a good breakfast.'

They chatted about their plans for the day over the meal and decided that with the aid of a camp table, they could both have a place to work. After she had finished her chores, she settled them both down and she began to draw again.

She was doing a series of monochrome sketches of animals to complement the full page coloured paintings for the other pages. It was very detailed and took her a great deal of time and concentration to get it right. She tried to ignore the bleeps and squeaks coming from Adam's computer and the rattle of his keyboard as he typed his messages.

'Blast,' he said at regular intervals. It appeared his new phone was working, but there was a few problems in transferring the information. 'I'll have to make some calls I'm afraid, hope it doesn't disturb you too much.'

'I don't suppose it will. I usually work to music but I thought that might be a bit too much with both of us here, besides, you'd probably hate the sort of stuff I listen to.' This led to a discussion about music and apart from a couple of deep disagreements, they were reasonably compatible in their tastes.

'Any chance of a coffee, now we've both broken off?' Adam asked.

'Why not? I'll put the kettle on. In fact, it's almost lunch time so I might as well make us a sandwich. Then we can both work through the afternoon.'

After the break, Adam began making phone calls. The third time Emily heard the saga of how he'd fallen down the slope and been rescued by the efficient Miss Tranter, a little thing you wouldn't think could lift a bucket of coal, she'd had enough. Her drawings weren't working and her concentration was quite impossible.

'I think I might need to work upstairs tomorrow,' she told him. 'I never realised just how much concentration I needed to put in to these pictures.'

'Sorry. I expect that's me going on. I needed to get people up to date with the situation, though. I'll just use e-mails for the rest of the day. I don't have to speak with them.'

'I wouldn't mind normally, but this is a bit of a deadline. It would be nice to have time to chat and not feel pressured.'

'There's so much I need to know about you, Emily Trantor. You're beautiful, talented and more patient than I could ever have wished for. I'd like to take you somewhere wonderful for a delicious meal. What do you think?'

'You need to get a bit more used to moving around on crutches before you make a public appearance anywhere that serves wonderful food. But yes, a meal out would be nice in a day or two.'

'You're very good to me. It's the least I can do. I hope you won't be offended if I pay the next grocery bill too. You must be on a pretty tight budget. And I still owe you for the taxi. I might have to give you a cheque if that's OK. I'm nearly out of cash.'

'I'll need to shop again tomorrow. It's only a small fridge so I can't buy much and we'll be out of fresh vegetables and bread. When do you have to go to the hospital again?'

'End of the week. Friday. I hope you can put up with me till then?' He reached for her hand and pressed his lips to it.

'I . . . I . . . of course you can stay.' She felt thoroughly confused by his touch. He may sound demanding and even a bit arrogant, but perhaps it was just his way of coping with a difficult situation. 'You're not used to being an invalid, are you?' she suggested. 'And maybe I should have my hand back?'

'If you insist. I can't tell you how frustrated I feel. If I could stand for more than two seconds, I would kiss you properly.'

'Adam, please. We hardly know each other. Apart from being stuck in the same place at the moment, I doubt there's anything we have in common. I can see from just the last couple of days, you are from a different social world altogether. Your car for a start. I bet I couldn't earn enough in three years to pay for that, even if I didn't buy anything else at all for those years.'

'I really don't see why you are so tetchy about it. What difference does it make? Most people would be glad that money isn't a problem. Besides, you have two homes, one in Cornwall. That isn't exactly someone who's living on the breadline.'

'This is an old family cottage, which is going to be sold anyhow. It's scarcely used at all now and my parents could do with an infusion of cash to make their lives easier.'

'Let's just forget about money and see what else we have in common.'

For the next half hour, they exchanged views on music, theatre, art, books, travel and eating out. They scored high points in agreement in most cases. When it came to travel, Emily's experience was very low.

'There's a lot of places I'd love to visit,' she said rather wistfully. 'We went to France a couple of times when we were little but as you'd guess, most holidays were spent down here.'

'So, you should make a wish list. Places you will visit when you can. Then you should work towards crossing them all off, one at a time.'

'And there speaks a man who has never encountered the words, *mortgage* or *rent* or *council tax*.'

'Now that's unfair. I have to work very hard at balancing books. Not my own, I grant you, but I spend my life dealing with financial matters. My father may own a string of stores, but he's a very keen businessman and I have to account for every penny we spend. What's the matter?'

He paused as Emily's jaw had dropped.

'Your father owns the entire string of Judd's stores?'

'Oh dear. I shouldn't have mentioned it, should I? Please don't let it come between us.'

'I'm sorry, but I'm afraid it does. I'll look after you for a day or two more and then you'll have to find somewhere else. Somewhere much more suitable for someone of your class.'

'But Emily . . . '

'So why are you called Bryant and not Judd?'

'Long story. But listen Emily, please. Forget all this nonsense about different classes. It's irrelevant. I'm still the same person you knew a few minutes ago. Nothing's changed.'

'Yes it has. Your family must be millionaires and here you are staying in an ancient cottage with limited facilities and working from a camp table.'

'For heavens sake. This is a charming place and if it hadn't been for your kindness and tenacity, well, who knows what could have happened? I like you very much and whether your parents were peasant workers on the land or related to royalty, it would really make no difference.'

'I'm sorry Adam. My mind is made up.'

5

'Please, Emily. Don't do this. I'm really enjoying being here with you and I'm sorry if I'm putting on you too much. Tell you what, I'll cook supper tonight. You get on with your work and I'll spoil you.'

'Don't be ridiculous. How can you cook with both hands holding on to your crutches?'

'I'll take that stool into the kitchen and I can sit on it to do most things. I'm quite inventive when it comes to it.'

She shrugged and nodded. Let him get on with it, she thought.

She settled back to work and tried to ignore the three calls that came to his mobile. It was difficult however and she began to admire the incisive way he dealt with matters that were obviously tricky. One call was slightly different.

'I'm sorry but that's impossible. No

. . . I have to go to the hospital on Friday . . . Yes, I know I could . . . No . . . I'm perfectly well looked after, thank you. Leave it, will you? Yes, you can send an e-mail. In fact, I'd prefer it . . . That's right. Bye.'

It was clear that someone was trying to persuade him to return to somewhere he could be better looked after. She worked on, interrupted by the dogs pushing their noses on to her knee.

'Go away, you two,' she murmured. 'We'll go out later when I've finished this drawing.' The Jack Russells gave a deep sigh as if they understood exactly what she'd said. They lay down again and kept their eyes fixed on her every movement.

'They know just what you're saying, don't they?' Adam remarked.

'Habit,' she muttered abstractedly. She continued to work, her hand movements sure and firm as she shaded the last part of the drawing.

'I do envy you your ability to draw. I used to try very hard, but everything came out looking like some strange mythical beast. Even when I was drawing a car.'

'You're undisciplined. Wrong sort of training. There. I think that'll do. That's about it for today.' The dogs immediately leapt up and began to dash around, whining and yapping.

'Talking of undisciplined . . . '

'I made them a promise and they know it's payback time. I'll put this lot away and then we'll go for our walk. Ready, girls?' They certainly were. 'Shall I put the stool ready for you?' she suggested as she was leaving.

'Thanks. I'll just finish this and then I'll make a start on supper.'

'You can cook, I presume?' she asked.

'Course. Nothing to it.'

She moved the stool and went off with the dogs. She went towards the sea this time, checking the state of the little bridge on her way. The boards had held firm and the stream was flowing rapidly along its normal course, leaving their route out of the property quite intact.

She crossed the road and walked along the narrow path. It was too late in the day to walk far and the February evening was closing in rapidly.

After the events of the past days, she decided not to take any risks and headed back. The dogs had been hoping for a romp on the beach and were clearly disappointed. She reflected on her strange situation. In a fit of pique, she had told Adam he must leave. Stupid pride, she realised. Why should she be ashamed of her background?

He had made it clear that he wanted to stay for a few days longer, at least until his hospital appointment at the end of the week. If she could manage to get her work done, there was no reason why he couldn't stay. Was there?

When she arrived back at the cottage there were definite cooking smells coming from the kitchen. There was chicken, she thought. Maybe potatoes . . . burning?

'Everything all right?' she asked.

'I think so. But the potatoes seem to be cooked. Well, a bit too cooked, maybe. Burned?'

'I thought I could smell something strange. What exactly are you making?'

'Chicken breasts boiled in wine.' Emily winced at the word, *boiled*. 'Sort of coq au vin, I suppose. It was going to be mashed potatoes, but I'm not sure now. And whatever vegetables I could find. There aren't many left, are there?'

'I told you I needed to shop again. Now, would you like me to see what I can rescue?'

'I'm useless, aren't I?'

'I thought you could cook.'

'So did I. There's obviously more to it than you'd think really, isn't there?'

'I guess so. I think those potatoes are a bit past rescue actually. We could have rice if you like it? And I'd better stop the chicken from boiling as you put it. You never boil meat. It makes it tough. You cook it gently. Simmer it.'

'I thought I'd better cook it quickly as the potatoes were ready.'

The next few minutes were spent in a sort of cookery lesson. He balanced awkwardly on the stool and insisted on doing his share of the work. Cleaning the burned pan almost brought him to submission, but he valiantly worked on it until it was clean enough to satisfy Emily's high standards.

'I just don't see how anyone manages to get everything cooked at the same time.'

'Practice,' she replied with a smile. 'You can have lessons for the rest of your time here.'

'Does that mean you're going to let me stay a bit longer?'

'Till your hospital visit anyhow. After that, we'll see what the prognosis is.'

He grabbed her hand and kissed it again. She couldn't help feeling flattered.

'Thank you so much. I'm really grateful. And I'll find a way to pay you back for your kindness. I think there may be lots of projects you could do for the stores.'

Emily smiled, wondering what on earth he could be thinking of, but more work would be useful, once she had finished her current assignment.

'I'm not sure you should be doing that,' she murmured, pulling her hand away from his lips.

'It's the only easy way of reaching you. If I stand up with the crutches, my arms are then busy.' He put on the little boy lost look which doubtless worked one hundred per cent with most women. But Emily steeled herself and refused to fall for it.

'Then I'm obviously much safer with you incapacitated, aren't I? Now, I'll clear away my stuff and set the table. You can bring yourself over here and pour the wine.'

As they ate, they discussed plans for the next few days. Emily made it clear that she would not be at his beck and call and that she needed to finish her work as quickly as possible. After supper, they played Scrabble again and this time he won handsomely.

'You know, I haven't played games like this since I was a kid. At that time, my mother had been feeling guilty about not pushing me into more educational games. I loathed it. So artificial to see my mother pretending to be a caring parent when really, all she wanted was to go to a bridge game or one of her endless treatments. Anyone setting up an alternative therapy centre knew they would make a fortune out of her.'

'Where is she now?'

'She died about four years ago.'

'I'm sorry . . . '

'Don't be. I'm quite over it. We were never really a close family. I was mostly looked after by a nanny or someone.'

Emily couldn't help thinking of the contrasts between them. Hers had been a happy romp of a childhood with scatty parents who often ignored meal times till they realised they were hungry. Their holidays had always been here in Cornwall, enjoying the scenery and beaches, whatever the weather.

Poor Adam, all the wealth and so-called privileges, had none of the closeness of family life.

★ ★ ★

The next morning, he insisted on giving her a cheque to pay for a load of shopping. She had gasped when she saw the amount and protested that she didn't need this much. He then gave her a list of things he'd like her to buy and she protested no longer. The list included several bottles of expensive wine and various foods that were usually way beyond her budget.

'I'd like to treat us a bit, if you don't mind cooking some of these things. I'm happy to buy them. I'm especially partial to duck and thought you might enjoy it, too.'

'Sorry, my meagre fare must have offended your gourmet palate.'

'Don't be silly. It's all been great. That isn't why I suggested it. I can't take you out for a meal at the moment and this is my best way of saying thank you for looking after me. I've loved everything you've cooked for me so far.'

'OK. I'll get off to the supermarket then. Shouldn't take too long. Do plenty of work while I'm away and thanks for the cheque. I appreciate it.'

'Take my car if you like. It's insured for anyone to drive.'

'Think I'll stick to my trusty old banger, thanks. I'd be mortified if I broke anything or dented it. Besides, the dogs can come with me. I'll give them a run on the beach before I do the shopping. Sure you've got all you need?' He nodded. 'Do you want me to make you a flask of coffee?'

'I'm sure I can manage that,' he said firmly.

As she drove along the narrow lanes and saw the gorse coming into full bloom, Emily considered her life. Though she was happy enough in her flat in Hertfordshire, she felt such a strong urge to spend much more time in Cornwall. If she could only raise enough money, she could sell the flat and maybe make her parents an offer on the house.

Just before they reached Penzance, Emily parked at a favourite cove and let the dogs out. It was still chilly, but the sun was shining and the dogs ran around, barking with delight and chasing each other madly round the deserted beach. At this time of year, there were few people about and their noise wasn't disturbing anybody.

Feeling her spirits lift, she chased with them, running wildly and shouting in the wind. This was total freedom and she felt exhilarated. She wondered if Adam might have enjoyed such freedom at any time. It would be fun to bring him here and share the wild beauty.

'Come on, you two. We must get on,' she shouted. Still rushing everywhere and barking, they followed her back. She rubbed them with the old towel she kept for the purpose and let them back into the car. They lay on the covered seat, panting as if they'd just run a marathon.

Once the shopping was finished, she drove back to the cottage, pleased to be leaving the town again. She must definitely consider her future and the possibility of living here. After all, with today's technology and the good postal service, why did she need to live near London? She turned on to the track and bumped carefully over the little bridge.

As she approached the cottage, she saw an expensive looking black car parked outside. It was not one she recognised. The dogs barked as they sensed another presence in their home.

Emily parked and got out. The dogs went to sniff the car and then ran to the door and waited for her to catch up with them. She collected several shopping bags and struggled to open the door, wondering who the visitor could be.

A tall elegant woman, possibly in her early thirties, was sitting next to Adam near the table. Her arm was pressed close to his and she gave the appearance of someone who was very familiar with the man and also a touch proprietorial.

'Hello,' Emily said a trifle nervously and clearly at a disadvantage. 'Sue, Snickett, get away.' Both dogs had stood sniffing at the newcomer and she had an expression of extreme distaste on her carefully made-up face. She felt a sense of hostility and even dislike towards the woman. She looked at Adam for an introduction.

'Hi, Emily. I see you bought up half the shops.'

'Only half. The rest's in the car.' The woman looked snootily at the heap of plastic carrier bags.

'Can't you get it delivered? But I suppose not, right out here in the sticks. Jemima Fairly,' she said holding out a hand so perfectly groomed Emily was afraid she might sully it by touching it. She had long immaculate fingernails, polished in a dark brownish colour to match her outfit and an elegant swept back hairstyle which immediately made her feel at a disadvantage.

'I'm Emily. Emily Tranter.'

'The woman who single-handedly saved my life,' Adam interjected. 'A version of superwoman and Mary Poppins combined.'

'You make me sound dreadful.' Emily giggled. 'Can I get you some coffee, Miss . . . er . . . Jemima?'

'Adam offered me some, but I don't think so, thanks. I rarely drink instant.' Her expression suggested she might be afraid of catching something nasty, 'Actually, I'm here to drive Adam back home. Perhaps you would be kind enough to pack his things for him? And bring them down to my car.'

'Excuse me, but I'm not here as a servant,' Emily protested. 'Besides. Adam didn't seem to want to leave when we talked about it earlier.'

'Well, it's clear you're hardly in a position to look after him properly. I mean, just look at the place. Hardly what he's used to and with no proper facilities.' Her voice took on a drawl which Emily found highly irritating.

'Actually, Jemima, she's right. I don't want to leave. It's taken me a lot of persuasion to get Em to agree to my staying on. I'm going back to the hospital on Friday, so there's no point leaving until after that.'

'But, darling, you can't possibly like being here. It's so poky and well, squalid.'

Emily thought she was about to burst with anger and took several deep breaths to steady her nerves.

'If you find it squalid, I suggest you leave as soon as possible. I don't know who you are exactly, but clearly nobody taught you any manners. This place is very dear to me and, in fact, I'm considering moving here permanently.' The look of shock on Jemima's face almost made her laugh aloud. She turned and went out to the car to fetch the rest of the shopping.

It had a dual purpose, not least that she needed to get away from that awful woman before she said something irrevocably rude. However rude she might have been already, she did not want to be reduced to the same level and start a slanging match. She couldn't help but wonder who the woman was. From the proprietorial way she was sitting so close to Adam, the implication was that they meant something to each other.

Despite herself, Emily felt more than a little jealous. She chided herself. Their meeting had been pure serendipity. If he hadn't been in such need at the time, they would never have met and never even stood a chance of becoming friends. Unable to stay outside any longer, she went back into her home, feeling desperately like some outsider who was visiting.

'Jemima's just leaving,' Adam informed her. The woman looked daggers at him and opened her mouth as if she was about to protest further. Angrily, she snapped her handbag shut and jingled her car keys.

'Really, Adam, I shall never fully understand you. You have a whole team of people who want very much to look after your every need and a splendid home with complete luxury. Instead you're choosing to stay in a tumbledown cottage in the middle of nowhere and virtually fend for yourself.'

She stared at him, waiting for a reply. When he said nothing, she shrugged. 'I can only gather there's more to all this than meets the eye.

'She's obviously got some hold on you that makes you want to stay here. Very well. I'll report to your father on the situation. He seemed adamant that we seek private specialists to deal with your injuries. You'll be hearing from him yourself, I expect. I doubt he'll be as tolerant of the situation as I have been. Goodbye, darling.'

'I think it's time you left,' Emily said far more calmly than she was feeling. 'I don't like your insinuations. I don't think I like you either, come to think of it. Adam's free to go at any time. In fact, go ahead. Make your arrangements and clear him out of my house and out of my life. I assure you, I should be glad to see him go if you are typical of the sort of friends he spends time with.'

Jemima glared as she gathered up her stylish leather coat and swung it over her shoulder. The dogs growled gently as she swept out of the room, slamming the door behind her.

'So, do you want to tell me what that was all about?' Emily demanded.

'That was Jemima, my father's personal assistant. She was sent down here . . . or at least, took it upon herself to come down to fetch me back. As you saw, I refused.'

'But why? As she said, you could be properly looked after in better surroundings and you'd have proper medical care all of the time. You might not have to learn to cook either.'

'I didn't want you to waste the duck.'

'How do you know I bought any duck?'

'Because I knew you would do all you could to get it. You want to please this poor sick man you've taken in. You did get some, didn't you?'

'Of course. Unless you decide you'd rather go back with Jemima. She's still outside, talking on her mobile phone. Is she your girlfriend?'

'She wishes. We've known her for years, of course. Daughter of a family friend. Dad took her on as his assistant as a favour, but she's actually quite good at the job and so she stayed. I've always been under pressure to make a match with her, but well, you saw how she is. Sensitive as a rhino. You can't force these things and well, I simply don't want to marry the woman.'

'Wow. Quite a deal, it seems. Must say, didn't take to her at all. I thought she was patronising, condescending and downright rude. As for her suggestion that something's going on between us . . . well! Sorry, I'm being rude myself now. I don't know anything about her really.'

'If I didn't know better, I might think you were a bit jealous.'

'Don't be ridiculous. Why should I be jealous? You're just someone who happens to be staying in my home. I'll unpack the shopping,' she said, 'and then heat up some soup. Only instant supermarket special, I'm afraid. The staff have the day off again. I really must get some work done this afternoon.'

'I'm sure it will be excellent. Whatever impression you may have got from Jemima, I'm really a very simple soul. No problems with instant foods. I eat them a lot of the time. When I'm busy, I don't have time to eat out.'

'Bet you shop much more upmarket than I do, whatever you say. Part cost, part convenience for me. Illustrators don't earn a great deal, you know.'

She busied herself putting away the shopping and her squirreling instincts were satisfied when she saw the fridge well stocked and the shelves of the cupboard filled. She also put several bottles of wine in the rack.

She had to admit, it had been nice to shop without considering the cost for once. She poured soup from a carton into a pan and set it to heat. There were fresh crusty rolls to have with it and some cheese.

'This is excellent soup,' Adam complimented her. 'Nicest I've tasted, for ready made. And great rolls. Really don't think Jemima should worry about me not being taken care of. She wouldn't do nearly such a good job. Mind you, she'd always know someone else to call upon.'

'I bet she would. I somehow don't think I've heard the last of Miss Jemima Fairly.'

6

All afternoon, Emily worked at her drawings. Every few minutes, she remembered the awful Jemima and felt herself heated by the anger from the morning's encounter. She pushed the dogs outside when she had finished and they looked very disappointed that there wasn't to be another walk.

'Go on, the pair of you. You had a lovely time on the beach this morning. It's supper time for us and I have to cook it.'

'I could peel the potatoes,' Adam offered.

'You sure? I mean to say, I don't want you to demean yourself with such a lowly task.'

'For goodness sake Emma. Let's call a truce. I'm very sorry that Jemima was so rude and I assure you, I'm nobody special. I'm not royalty or even the sort of person she seems to think I am. I've really enjoyed these few days . . . except perhaps, for the pain and inconvenience. Now, where are these spuds? Let me get at them. What are we having, by the way?'

'I assumed you'd want the duck you asked me to buy. How do you like it cooked?'

'I've no idea.'

'OK. I'll pan fry it with a little garlic and make a sauce with some cream and the juices.'

'Sounds like heaven. Thank you.' Yet again, he caught her fingers and made a great play of kissing them. 'When I can stand unaided, I shall kiss you properly,' he said firmly. Emily felt herself blushing once more and pulled her hand away.

'Please don't, Adam. I like you very much, but let's face it, we simply don't have a future together. I'd be terrified of meeting your father and as for fitting a social scene with the likes of your Jemima, well, I'm a total nonstarter.'

'She's not my Jemima. But as I've been trying to tell you, I'm a non-starter too. I hate all this superficial social stuff. Playing Scrabble with you is much more my scene. I never really realised what a rude and inconsiderate woman she is till today. I saw her in a totally new light. Right. I've finished the potatoes. What's next?'

'You can prepare the runner beans.'

'Oh Lord. How do I do that? Wouldn't you rather do them to make sure they're done how you like them?'

'I shall demonstrate on one and you can do the rest.'

'You're a hard task master. OK. Go for it. Show me how to prepare a bean.'

In many ways, Jemima's visit had been a turning point in the relationship between them. They had reached a companionable ease together and Emma wondered if she wasn't falling just a tiny bit in love with this handsome man who was sharing her home. Her common sense told her it was not a sensible move.

As she had said to him earlier in the day, he was simply someone who needed help and she had offered it. She felt that she was seeing a side of him that most people were unaware existed. They laughed together over simple things and even the task of cooking gave a great deal of pleasure.

'So, who taught you how to cook?' Adam asked.

'I suppose my mum did. Though it was more a case of us helping her and learning as we went along. My brother's just as good a cook as I am.'

'Lucky him. I think everyone should learn. Though if I'd been waiting for my mum to teach me, I'd have been unlucky. Well, I was I guess. We usually had someone living in who did the meals and then I was at an all male boarding school, so there never was much opportunity. Show me what you're doing with the duck. It might be a useful dish for me to make for myself.'

'Or for entertaining Jemima to a nice

intimate dinner sometime?'

'I told you. There will never be any nice intimate dinners with her. I agree with you. I think I'm beginning to dislike her myself. After today's little show, I think she's proved what a nasty piece of work she can be.'

Emma smiled, feeling ridiculously pleased by his words. But maybe there was someone else in his life? Not that she could consider herself to be any sort of serious contender, but it would be nice to know what she might be up against.

'So, if Jemima's out of the running, who else might there be lurking in the shadows?'

'Nobody really. I never seem to have enough time to meet people and settle down. I'm always travelling somewhere. Overseas and all over the country. Doesn't make it easy to establish any sort of relationships. In fact, this is probably the longest I've spent in the company of one person for several years. I'm rather enjoying it actually. If it wasn't for this stupid leg . . . '

'If it wasn't for the stupid leg, you wouldn't be here in the first place and certainly not staying here under any other circumstances.'

'Incidentally, did you mean what you said about moving here permanently?'

'I'm thinking about it. I love being here and don't like my flat at home much. I don't really have to be near London . . . with the ease of communication these days, as you said yourself. Once I learn to use a computer, I don't see why I can't continue with a few trips a year to meet up with people. I'd have to raise quite a lot of money though. My parents wanted to sell to realise some capital and my brother will also expect his share, so it won't be cheap. I can sell the flat of course, but that won't be nearly enough.'

'You'll just have to get a nice lucrative contract with someone and then your problems will all be over.'

'Oh yes. Contracts fall off trees, do they?'

'I told you. I'm sure we can put some work your way. And we would certainly be generous. I'll see what I can do.'

'Please. I don't want any favours, but it does sound interesting. Right. I think this is ready now.'

She drained the vegetables and dished up the fragrant meat. Adam tucked in hungrily and said it was as good as any meal he'd eaten anywhere. They had a good bottle of claret to accompany it and both felt comfortable and relaxed. Emily had lit candles and the soft light gave the old cottage a warm glow and enhanced the atmosphere of cosiness.

'I can understand why you might choose to live here. The dogs are happy and it's very peaceful. Not always convenient perhaps, but there's a really good feel to it.'

'As long as there isn't a power cut and someone gets stuck halfway down a ravine.'

'True, but all that simply proved your versatility.' He reached out and took her hand. His eyes glowed darkest brown and he pressed her finger tips to lips once more. 'I hope we can see each other when I can walk properly again and return home. I'd like to find some way of thanking you properly.'

'There's no need for that, I assure you, but, it might be nice to meet up occasionally and maybe have a meal.'

'Does that mean you are still trying to keep me at arms length?'

'I'm trying to be practical. We live in different worlds. You said so yourself, you're always off travelling somewhere and don't have time to spend getting to know anyone. Besides, your father is obviously reliant on you and probably has very clear ideas of who you should spend time with and eventually settle down with.'

'He doesn't make those sort of decisions for me, I assure you. Otherwise he'd have had me settled with Jemima and producing dozens of heirs by now. No, the nice thing about being here is that I am a normal human being and nobody special. That's all I am, of course, but everyone seems to think they have to treat me with kid gloves because of what my father stands for. Now, isn't it about time you kissed me properly? Come and sit next to me. I'm sure that even with my leg stuck on a stool, there has to be some way we can manage it.'

Shyly, Emily moved closer. She leaned towards him. His lips brushed hers and she closed her eyes and she felt something she recognised as love, sweeping over her. It was so unexpected that she didn't give herself time to check and stop it right away. She truly wanted this moment to last forever. Time could stop right now and she would feel endlessly happy. Adam drew away and she felt bereaved.

She opened her eyes again and looked at him, wondering if he was disappointed in her response. He clearly didn't feel the way she was feeling.

'Sorry,' he muttered. 'Cramp.' They

both burst out laughing. 'I told you I wasn't quite my usual self.'

'Then maybe it's all for the best. We can't possibly have any sort of future so it's best we leave it right now.'

'But I don't want to.'

'I'm sorry. It has to be this way. I need it to be this way. I can't afford to develop any more feelings for someone like you. This is just one short time that our paths have crossed and we are both going our separate ways very soon. You'll doubtless make someone a wonderful husband when the time is right.'

'Hey . . . whoa there. I'm not making any suggestions here. I just like your company . . . I'm not suggesting life-long commitment.'

'Of course not, but I'm not the sort of person who can consider any sort of relationship with someone I can't trust one hundred percent. I can't afford to be hurt or to give anyone false impressions of what I'm really like. Now, I'm sorry if you thought I was giving out the wrong message, but it's time I cleared away the supper things and went to bed.'

'Emily, stop. I'm not saying I don't want us to get to know each other better. It takes time. Please, stop clattering those dishes and sit down again. Listen to me.'

'I think I've heard all I need to hear. Sorry Adam. I'm tired and I must be up early tomorrow to get my work done. I'm still way behind.' She felt rather closer to tears than she wanted. She'd made an idiot of herself and given quite the wrong impression of what she really meant. Now she had ruined everything and the sooner he left her to get on with her own life the better it would be for all concerned.

As she took the dirty dishes into the kitchen she saw his face. He looked shocked and his mouth had become a firm set line. His dark eyes were unfathomable in the dim light. She couldn't read exactly what he was thinking but assumed he realised he'd had a narrow escape. What she wanted to do more than anything else was to take him in her arms and show him her true feelings. But this was moving into what was far too dangerous territory and she must remove herself from such temptation.

'Right. I'll just let the dogs out for the final time and then I'll be off to bed. Anything else you need?'

'Emily, please. I don't want you to have the wrong impression. I simply don't think I'm ready to settle down. You said yourself, we don't know each other well enough yet, but I'd like to remedy that. I'm not saying you aren't the right one for me . . . you could very well be. It's just too soon to tell. We've only known each other a few days.'

'Precisely. For heaven's sake, Adam. I'm not asking you to marry me. I was trying to point out that I'm not getting involved seriously with you or anyone else until I am certain it is the right thing to do.'

'Good. Seems we are agreed then.

But . . . ' He stared at her face which was now impassive. 'OK. I'll be out of your hair once I've been to the hospital on Friday. Just let's get through tomorrow and I'll see what I can arrange.'

'Excellent. Come on Sue, Snickett. Out you go.'

She finished washing up and put the dry crockery away. The little kitchen was neat and tidy, but she busied herself wiping round the surfaces once more.

'You go on up. I think you can probably manage by yourself now, can't you? You can use the bathroom first and I'll be up later.'

He looked troubled but rose and called goodnight as he worked his way up the stairs. When she went to bed herself, she called a soft goodnight back to him. She slept badly and kept waking up with the feeling that something was wrong.

As she remembered the rather silly scene the previous evening, she felt a great sense of disappointment that she had spoiled everything. He had surely misinterpreted what she meant, but whatever the reason, nothing would be quite the same again.

It was raining heavily the next morning and the dogs were pushed outside without their beloved mistress accompanying them. They were reluctant to expose themselves to the wet and sat shivering pathetically on the doorstep.

'What a pair of wimps,' Emily called to them. 'Go and do what dogs have to do,' she told them. Eventually, she had to give in and let them back inside. She rubbed them dry with old towels and talked to them as she did so. 'You're nothing but a pair of babies.' She swung round as she heard the stairs creak.

'Hi. How are you today?' Adam asked.

'Fine. And you?'

'OK. Didn't sleep too well.'

'Must have been the rain starting. It kept me awake too.'

'Pity. If we'd known we were both awake, we could have had a game of Scrabble.'

'Seems like you've become a convert. You ready for breakfast?'

'Great. Thanks.'

They held a stilted conversation over breakfast, both of them feeling the tension of their exchanges of the previous evening.

'Emily . . . ' he began. 'I wanted to say . . . '

'Don't say anything, Adam. I'm only sorry it had to turn out this way. We'll have to make some arrangement to get you taken home after the hospital tomorrow. Is there someone who could come and drive you and your car back?'

'I don't know. I expect so.'

'Good. Then you can get it sorted today.'

'If that's what you really want.'

'It is. I have a lot to do and I'm running out of time.'

As soon as breakfast was over, Emily set out her work and began to concentrate on her drawings. Adam typed away on his laptop and was sending messages. He apologised a couple of times when he needed to make phone calls and spoke briefly and as quietly as he could. Several times Emily was tempted to change her mind about letting him stay on, but resisted and listened as he tried to make his arrangements.

It was almost lunchtime when a call came for him. This time he didn't speak quietly but, was at times almost shouting. Whatever was being said, clearly angered him.

With only one side of the conversation, it was difficult to guess who was on the other end but she had thought at first it was Jemima. She stopped drawing and listened to the angry words.

'That is quite unjustified. I don't care. It is not true. You can't make these judgements.' Each sentence was followed by a pause as the person on the other end had his say. She could only guess what slanders were being put forward. The conversation was drawing to a close. 'If you insist . . . I dare say . . . if that's what you want . . . Very well. Ten o'clock . . . Yes . . . OK . . . I'll see you later then.' He snapped off the phone and looked very tense.

'OK. So are you going to tell me what that was all about?' Emily asked.

'You don't want to know.'

'Maybe not. But you're going to tell me.'

'That was my father. When Jemima got back last night, she told him that you were virtually keeping me a prisoner here and yes, the word *squalid* was used again. She told him that you were obviously in it for whatever money you could get out of it and would probably refuse to let me leave until you were properly repaid.'

'I'll write you a cheque to repay the money you gave me for the shopping. I didn't want to take it in the first place.'

'Don't be ridiculous. I owed you heaps for the taxi anyhow and you must not take any notice of their nasty comments. Jemima is only trying to get back at me for turning her down. Sadly Dad will never hear a word said against her, but, the upshot is, he's sending one of the men down on the overnight train. He'll get here in time to collect me and drive me back home after the hospital appointment. Wanted to rescue me today, but I insisted on keeping my appointment tomorrow. At least it gives us the chance for one last evening together and the chance of my last cookery lesson, maybe?'

Emily stared at his handsome face. How dare his father make such dreadful comments and why hadn't Adam stood up to him? Defended her much more vehemently? True he had protested slightly, but in the face of such obvious lies, he should have said so much more.

Still, he was obviously somewhat in awe of his father so maybe it was just simple fear, but perhaps she shouldn't be judgemental. She had no idea what his father was really like, after all.

'I can't believe anyone could be so

rude. How dare your father make assumptions when he doesn't know anything about me? And you didn't exactly defend me did you?'

'You don't argue with my father. Whatever he says is gospel and arguing simply makes him even more certain he's right. I'm sorry, but I do know when it's worth saying anything and when it's pointless. He's been fed lies by Jemima and because he's naturally so prejudiced, I didn't even try to argue. Besides, you wanted me out of your hair and it happened to coincide with your request. But, do I get my cookery lesson tonight or not?'

Despite her anger, Emily couldn't help but smile. One thing she felt sure of, remaining outside the Bryant family was a good move. No way should she be involved with people like that. Her own family may not have all the wealth of Adam's, but there was a great deal of love between them all. However nice it must be to have unlimited wealth, she'd rather have her own family any day.

7

Despite her confused emotions, Emily worked hard all afternoon and managed to complete a number of her drawings.

'Excellent,' she muttered. 'Just one more big one to do and that's it.' She was really speaking to herself, but Adam lifted his head.

'Well done. So how much longer will it take?'

'Probably only another couple of days. I have it all roughed out and the sheet blocked and stretched. Then I'll go back to civilisation. After the weekend I expect. I'd like to have a day or two to enjoy Cornwall without pressure.'

'Sounds wonderful. I wish I could stay on and enjoy it with you.' He sounded wistful. It was almost a question and she was tempted to accept.

'You've got a chauffeur coming down to take you back tomorrow.'

'Actually, no. I've just sent a message to my father to tell him to cancel it. There's no way I can sit in my car for several hours at this stage. You know what it's like. Built for fit and healthy people and not someone with a crook leg. If you really don't want me to stay with you, I'll have to book myself into the hotel again. Now I'm a bit more mobile, I should be able to manage, but you must realise I'd much rather be here with you and the dogs.'

'Thought you didn't like dogs much.'

'These two are different. Look at them, sitting cuddled up in a dog heap. I'll miss them tremendously.'

'So, if you do stay on, how will you organise the hospital trip and possibly follow-up physiotherapy. They're sure to suggest it.'

'I wondered if you would consider helping me? I'd make sure you weren't out of pocket.'

Emily felt her temper rising.

'You won't buy me. If I do help you it will be because I want to and not because you're paying me. How dare you? I suppose it's your way of doing everything, paying for it.'

'Please Emily. I was merely suggesting that I'd buy some groceries and pay for the odd tank of petrol if you drove me anywhere. I value your friendship and want it to continue. I certainly didn't mean to offend you in any way.'

'I'm sorry. I suppose I'm a bit sensitive and well, knowing who you are. I'm aware of being inadequate. Your father is obviously convinced that I'm trying to get money out of you.'

'Forget my father, Jemima and everyone else. This is between us. I'd love to stay on with you for a bit longer. I'll probably need to visit the hospital a couple of times more, but I'm sure we could have some time together without my being a burden to you. Please Emily. At least think about it.'

'I'm going to take the dogs for a walk. I'll consider it while I'm out.'

'Thank you. Thank you so much. You won't regret it. I'll be a model patient and perfect house-guest.'

'I haven't said yes. I've said I'll think about it.'

* * *

It was still blustery as she set off along the path towards the sea. She pulled her hood up tight and trudged along the wet track. The dogs ran here and there, as always and barked at the wind, leaping and bounding happily. Emily's mind was bouncing in equal measure.

One minute she wanted Adam to stay on and to have the chance to share with him some of her favourite places in the area. At other times, she felt the fear of letting him grow too close to her.

Her heart wanted him to be closer, but her brain told her it was dangerous to allow it. How often did a person meet someone like this man? If she sent him packing, she might regret it for the rest of her life. If he stayed it would be so much more difficult when it ended.

It was sure to end once he was back in his normal routine, doing all the things he took for granted . . . like flying first class all over the world for instance. How on earth might she cope with that sort of lifestyle?

But, there she was, making assumptions again. He had suggested nothing more than friendship, even a close one maybe. She was looking on it as a permanent relationship leading to marriage and that was just plain silly. But, it was how she was. She could never have a casual affair with anyone, however much she liked them. Maybe this was the problem. Maybe this was exactly what Adam was expecting.

When she finally reached the beach, it was even more blustery with the wind tugging at her anorak and waves crashing over the rocks sending up huge plumes of spray. The dogs scampered around and kept returning to Emily to make sure she wasn't leaving without them.

'Come on, girls. This isn't much fun, is it?' The little dogs followed her and they set off back down the track. 'Shall we let Adam stay or make him go?' she asked them. Tails wagged at the sound of her voice. 'I reckon that's a yes, isn't it?'

The decision made, she walked quickly back to the cottage. When she pushed the door open, she heard Adam's voice raised as he was arguing with someone on the phone. She dried the dogs and peeled off her wet clothes and boots.

'Too bad,' Adam was shouting. 'No. I've made my decision. Emily is a lovely lady. Warm and generous and nothing remotely like any of the superficial people I've known all my life. I am staying in Cornwall, either here or at a hotel. If Jones comes down, I shall send him back. No. I'm quite sure. Bye Dad.'

'Have you finished?' Emily asked tentatively.

'Quite finished. One rather angry

parent there. It's about time I stood up for myself.'

'I quite agree, and yes, you can stay here. I'll take you to the hospital tomorrow and then we'll spend the day together. You can take me out for lunch as you once suggested and I'll work very hard on Saturday. After that, we'll see what happens. OK?'

'You sound very forceful. I like it. Have we got something you can teach me to cook for supper?'

'I thought we'd have fish pie.'

'Fish pie?' he echoed in horror. 'I haven't eaten that since I was at school.'

'My special recipe. Using fresh salmon and a few prawns. You wanted to be treated like a normal human being. Normal humans eat fish pie.'

'OK. If you say so. Sounds awful, but I guess you know what you're doing. Does your pie need some potatoes peeling?' She nodded and handed him the peeler and a couple of potatoes. He did the job quickly and efficiently. 'What's next?'

'You need to cook the salmon. Microwave's best.' She showed him how to wash and skin the fish and added seasoning and lemon juice. Making the sauce was slightly more tricky as he didn't realise he needed to stir it continuously and it went lumpy. 'It's OK. Use the whisk. That should rescue it.'

They worked together and produced a tasty meal. Adam seemed to enjoy the process of cooking and thoroughly enjoyed the product at the end.

'That was excellent. Not a bit like the fish pie I remember. I've never done anything like this before. I'd like to try other things. Do you think we can?'

She laughed at his enthusiasm and agreed they might try something more ambitious another day. It was a happy evening and she felt content that she would have a few more days of his company.

★　★　★

They were up early the next morning in preparation for the hospital trip. They agreed that Emily's car might be more comfortable for him as it was easier to get in and out. She left the dogs behind, much to their disgust and drove the ten miles or so to Penzance. While Adam was being attended to, she went to collect more shopping to last for the weekend. When she arrived back at the hospital, Adam was waiting outside with just a walking stick and only an elastic support on his leg.

'They're very pleased with me. Evidently I show remarkable healing properties and all I have to do now is exercise and rest between. All your expert nursing has paid off. Seems the injuries weren't as bad as they first thought.'

'So you'll soon be fit enough to drive home.'

'Maybe, but what it mostly means is that we can enjoy a few days exploring. I want to see something of the Cornwall you are so fond of. My own experience of it is rather limited. One good walk in the pouring rain and one evening spent in a deep gully. Now, where are we going for lunch?'

'There's a lovely little pub near here. Good food and a friendly landlord.'

'Let's go then.'

They sat in the old country pub and enjoyed an excellent meal. It gave them the chance to talk a great deal and discover much more about each other. Emily realised this was probably the first time she had ever spent so long alone with a man.

She wondered what her parents, or indeed, anyone else might think about her sharing her home with someone like him. Who cared what anyone thought? She knew exactly how she felt about him and above all, believed that she could trust him.

They drove back to the cottage and she settled down to a little work. Adam busily carried out the exercises shown to him at the hospital. He was a model visitor, quiet while she worked and attentive when she stopped. He took a gentle walk outside and watched the dogs cavorting round the little garden.

The sun returned and the air was warm again. There had been no more communication with his father or the office and he felt relaxed and at ease. When he saw that Emily was packing up work for the day, he made her a drink and they sat together on the stone bench outside the back door.

'It's getting a bit cold. Don't want you to catch a chill,' she said, 'or I'll never get rid of you.' He pulled a face as he got up. He hobbled inside and put more logs on the fire.

'That should soon get you warm again. So, what culinary delight do you have planned for this evening?'

'I'm still full from lunch. How about an omelette?'

'Sounds great. There's a film I'd fancy watching this evening. What do you think?'

To Emily, it sounded like a cosy couple sort of arrangement. There were subtle changes in the mood and she sensed that he was making a huge effort to fit in with her lifestyle and to make sure that he wasn't being a nuisance in any way. She found it rather endearing. Perhaps standing up to his father had done something for him. Broken some sort of mould. Though she had work to do, she was looking forward to the next day or two.

By the Sunday, Adam was feeling ready to take a short walk. They drove to a nearby lighthouse and walked along the cliff path a little way, where the ground was reasonably level. The gorse was in full bloom, filling every corner with brilliant golden flowers, even though it was only February. The sun was shining on the lighthouse, reflecting the brilliant white paint.

'It's so bright you can hardly look,' Adam said. 'The sea is so intensely blue, it rivals the Mediterranean. Yes, you're right. This place is very special. Just a little further then I'll be ready to sit down.'

'You're doing very well. I'm beginning to think you're a bit of a fraud. I think you could easily have managed the journey back. Come on. Admit it.'

'Maybe. But I didn't want to go. I wanted to stay here with you. I like your company and I really did want to see something of the area. But you're right. I will have to leave soon. I'm not sure I can manage to drive myself yet.'

'I'll need to go back soon. I've almost finished the book and I'll have to start looking out for some more work. There will be another book eventually, but I need something to move on to next.'

'I was thinking about that. We need some new publicity material designing. We have themed promotions throughout the stores. Window and counter displays. Leaflets. Posters. You know the sort of thing. How would you feel about doing some designs for us?'

'Surely you have companies to do that for you? Or in-house artists?

'Well, yes, but there's Easter coming soon and seeing what you've done with those animal drawings, well, I'd like a completely different style for us for once. We could get some cards done specially. Things to give away to kids etc.'

'You're pushing it a bit. Easter isn't that far away. Not much time to get everything approved and printed. What sort of lead time are you thinking of?'

'We have our own printers. They'll put it together very fast. As for our own designers, well, they're totally stuck in a time warp. It's time we got new thinking in the company.'

'I can hardly see your father approving anything I suggest. This wicked woman who's keeping you a prisoner in such squalor.'

'He doesn't have to know it's you,' replied Adam with a glint in his eye. 'I can tell him that I've discovered an artist living in Cornwall and didn't want to return until I'd signed her up for the company.'

Emily considered his words and admitted to feeling excited by the proposals. If nothing else, it would certainly tide her over until a new book commission came up and it would be something quite different. Enlarge her range of expertise.

On the other hand, he was making assumptions that may not happen, so she couldn't afford to get too excited.

'Sounds great, but we need to see what they say.'

'I think I've had enough walking for one day. Let's see if we can find somewhere that does a cream tea. That's what it's famous for around here isn't it?'

'Very unhealthy, but we may find somewhere open. Most places close down for the winter, but you never know your luck.'

* * *

The next few days were spent very happily. Emily drove Adam round to see her favourite haunts and he managed a few short walks to the less

132

accessible places. He was captured by the simple beauty of cliffs and headlands and watching sea birds soaring into clear blue skies. He even tried to drive his car a few times but it was not easy.

He spent an hour or two each day using his computer and mobile phone, keeping up with office matters. While Emily was working one day, she overheard a conversation that made her feel less happy. He was speaking softly and smiling as he did so.

'No. Of course I've missed you.' He laughed. 'In a couple of days maybe. OK. I'll see you then.'

She pretended she hadn't been listening, but it was clear that he was speaking to someone he was fond of and arranging to see when he returned. Feelings of jealously returned to her mind. He did have a friend of some sort that he was pleased to meet again. Jemima? She thought not after all he had said.

'What's up?' he asked later.

'Nothing. Why should there be?'

'You just seem a bit tense.'

'Just busy.' He was staring at her. 'What?' she muttered.

'I just wondered why you looked so crabby.'

'I couldn't help overhearing your call. Jemima?'

'Of course not. It was my secretary.'

'On a Saturday?'

'She wanted to sort out some stuff I'd sent her. It's OK. She's at least fifty. A lovely lady who looks after me better than my own mother ever did.'

'You sounded very fond of her.'

'Of course I am. Like I said, she's a mother to me. Spoils me rotten and I like to respond.'

Emily had to believe him but it did show her how little she really knew about him. She was not going to let jealousy, especially needless jealousy, spoil the last of their time together.

All too soon, their brief holiday came to an end. Emily was due to take her artwork back to London to deliver to the publishers.

As he didn't feel confident to drive the long distance home, Adam's father arranged for his driver to fetch him back. As Adam had instigated the journey himself, he was happy that his father knew it was his own decision and that he had not been influenced.

'This has been a very special few days,' Adam told her. 'I think I've learned a lot about myself as well as getting to know you. I'll let you know about the work as soon as I've cleared it with the directors and we'll get together to discuss the whole package. I'll call you and maybe you can come and stay with me for a few days.'

'Let's see how it goes, eh?' Emily could feel herself near to tears and it simply would not do to show Adam how she was feeling. She had admitted to herself during the night, when she was tossing and turning, that she was more than a little in love with this man. This same man she had thought so impossible when they had first met.

It had been a short time, but the concentration of spending most of the days together meant that she had come to know him far better than she had ever known any of her previous boyfriends. She would miss those dark eyes and the boyish grin when he was pleased with something. She would miss everything about him.

In truth, she didn't really expect she would hear from him again, but she could always hope. If she was her usual sensible self, she would try to forget all about him. He was out of her reach and his world was far and away from her world.

'I'll be glad to get a few more clothes to wear. This sweater is about ready to walk out on its own,' he grumbled as he put his few belongings in his bag. 'Looks like the taxi coming up the track. Can we offer Jones some coffee?'

'Course. But I expect you'll want to get on your way soon. It's a long drive and I need to get off myself. Just got to make sure everything's turned off and safe.' She put the kettle on and swallowed hard to keep herself calm. She could still feel her emotions on the brink of collapsing. She refused to make a complete fool of herself.

'Hello. Welcome to Cornwall,' she said to the driver as he came inside the cottage.

'Good day, Miss. Sir. Hope you're feeling better, sir.'

'Much better thanks, Jones. Thought you'd appreciate a coffee before we got on the way.'

'Very kind, sir. Thank you.'

Emily grimaced as she made the coffee. She hated the deferential way he spoke.

'How do you like it? Milk, sugar?'

'White and one sugar, thanks Miss.'

'Please, call me Emily. I can't do with such formality.'

'Thank you Miss . . . Emily.' The man was clearly ill at ease.

'You want some coffee, Adam?'

'Just a small one.'

She handed him a cup and their fingers brushed as she did so. She felt a tremor run through her body and his fingers held hers for a brief moment. Their eyes met and she almost spoke her thoughts aloud. His eyes flicked towards Jones and she remained silent.

After so long alone with him, it was ironic that she now felt like speaking, just when there was an audience. Perhaps it was for the best that she didn't make a fool of herself.

All too soon, they were ready to go. Jones sat in the driving seat of Adam's car and his bag was loaded in the boot.

'Goodbye, Emily. And thank you so much for all your care and hospitality. I won't forget these days. They have been very special.' He leaned forward and kissed her softly on the lips. She felt as if she might sink to the ground, such was the intensity of her feelings.

'Goodbye Adam. It's been lovely ... I mean ... safe drive.' She was burbling like an idiot.

'I'll be in touch soon. Safe drive to

you too. Bye dogs. Be good.'

And that was it. He disappeared from view. She went back inside and washed the cups. The cottage felt empty and her heart felt equally empty. Though she knew it was all for the best, she missed him already.

She plumped the cushions which still bore the imprint of his body. She'd washed the sheets already and spread them over a rack to dry. Routine chores. Closing the cottage for a few weeks till someone else decided to visit. Would her parents really sell it? This could be the last time she visited this dear place she'd known all her life. Maybe she would be able to buy it. Decisions.

'Come on, dogs. I've done enough moping around. Let's hit the road.'

8

Back in her flat in Hertfordshire, she resumed her mundane life. She called a few friends and they met up for drinks in a local wine bar. Her best friend, Michelle, asked her what was wrong.

'Nothing,' Emily protested. 'I'm just a bit tired. I've been working pretty hard and drove back yesterday.'

'You don't seem your usual bright bouncy little self. Are you ill, in love or just moping?'

'No to all three,' she lied. 'Now, tell me all the gossip. What's been going on while I've been incarcerated in my lonely cottage? Don't forget I've been cut off from civilisation for a couple of weeks.'

'Nobody to talk to except your dear little dogs. Did you get troubled by the storms? It made the news here. I nearly rang you, but I knew you hate to be disturbed when you're working.'

'Well, we did have a powercut for a couple of days. And we were cut off by floods.'

'Wow. I assume it's the royal we?'

'Well, me and the dogs.' She felt herself blushing.

'Emily Tranter. You're not telling me the whole truth here. Come on, I know you too well.'

They were interrupted by the arrival of two more friends and she was spared further interrogation.

'I'll hear all about it later,' Michelle whispered. 'You're not off the hook yet, you know.'

'What's this? Secrets from your friends?'

But soon, they were all chatting about their lives and offices and Emily escaped without telling anyone about her few days with Adam. It was how she wanted it to be, she thought. She wasn't ready to share her little adventure yet. It was too special and too private.

'I'm going to London tomorrow,'

Emily said with a yawn. 'I have an appointment with my agent in the morning and have to catch the early train. I think I'll call it a night.'

'But you haven't told us about your stay in Cornwall,' protested Michelle.

'Nothing to tell. I was working.'

'So you say. We'll meet up again at the weekend, shall we? There's a good band on at The Smithy on Saturday night.' They all agreed to meet again and Emily called goodnight as she left.

The train ride to London seemed endless, though it was a familiar route. Her large portfolio was cumbersome and she was forced to hold it rather than stow it anywhere. Once she arrived at her agent's office, things improved.

'Em, these are gorgeous. Best you've done. They'll be absolutely thrilled, I'm sure. You've captured exactly the right tone with the drawings. Well done, darling.'

'I'm glad you like them. When will you know if the publishers like them?'

'We could hop into a taxi and take

them over right away if you like.'

'OK. Let's do it. I could do with the money as soon as possible. And I need to get on with the next project. Have you got anything lined up for me?'

'You know what the market's like at the moment. Very little around. I'll do my best for you. Once they see this little lot, I'm sure there'll be something else very soon. You could try putting an exhibition together?'

'I don't work that way. You know I don't. Never mind, something may turn up. I can always do posters for the Scout jumble sale,' Emily said far more cheerfully than she was feeling. Maybe Adam would turn up with the contract he mentioned. Maybe pigs might fly, she thought realistically.

The trouble was, whatever she was thinking and wherever she was, Adam crept into her thoughts. She could remember every detail of his handsome face. The way his hair curled into the back of his neck. His gorgeous dark eyes. The way his mouth crinkled when he smiled.

She also forced herself to think about his bad temper during the first days. The way he bossed her about and asked her to do things when he could see she was busy.

She also gave thought to his seemingly overbearing family and the way his father had ordered him back. Jemima and her rudeness and patronising attitude. He was out of reach and needed to stay that way.

'So, are you ready, darling? Put the drawings back in your case and we'll be on our way.'

'Sorry, I was miles away. I'm ready, David, really.'

'If I didn't know you better I'd swear you were in love or something equally silly. You're hardly here with me, are you, darling?'

'Guess I'm just tired. It's been quite a few days.'

★ ★ ★

The publishers were indeed delighted with her work and accepted it all without any changes. They promised to send her a cheque at the end of the following week.

'We'll be in touch when we want something else. Nothing in the pipeline at the moment, but I'm sure we shall want to use you again. Wonderful work.'

She took the train home and was greeted by her ecstatic dogs. Her neighbour usually let them out into her tiny garden when she was away for a day, but they still made her feel very guilty for leaving them for so long. She tidied the already tidy flat, put some washing into the machine and finally took the dogs for a walk in the dark.

It wasn't like walking in Cornwall. Here, it was a walk along the roads. She made a decision and planned to call her parents when she got back.

'Hi, Mum. How are you? Yes, I'm back safely.'

'How's the cottage at this time of year? Did you freeze? Oh, and we heard the power was off. Did that affect you? How did you cope?'

Typical of her mum, Emily thought. Strings of questions and never waiting for an answer.

'Listen, Mum, I was wondering if you've made any final decision about selling Tranter's?'

'Well, your father and I could do with selling it. It will be a dreadful wrench, of course, but well, family holidays won't realistically happen any more, will they? We could get a decent price for it and that would make all the difference to us now. We'd give you both a share, of course. Might help you, too.'

'The thing is, well . . . what do you think you might get?'

She named a price that made Emily gasp with horror. Even if she got an equally high price for her flat and took her share into the equation, it was more than she could ever be able to raise.

'Why do you ask?'

'I was wondering if it might be

possible for me to buy it. Move down permanently. But I'd never raise that amount of money.'

'Why on earth would you want to lock yourself away down there?'

'I love it so much. Now I'm home . . . well, I'd just rather be there. I can work better there. I don't need to be near London at all.'

'I see. Well, I don't know what to say. Of course you should have it if you want it, but . . . well, there's Simon to consider and we did rather hope to have some extra capital to live on. Your father and I were hoping to see a bit of the world before it's too late.'

'Of course you do. Forget it. It was only a pipe dream. Just an idea. So, where do you plan to go?'

The rest of the conversation was spent in hearing exotic plans for travelling the world and seeing places Emily had barely heard of. She tried to be enthusiastic for her mother's sake, but she was far too worried about her own future to take everything in.

Maybe she should consider taking some part-time job until something came up. She could always work in a bar or a shop, anything to keep paying the bills.

After a whole week had passed without any contact from Adam, she tried desperately to push him out of her thoughts. Each time she tried to move on, she remembered something he'd done or said and wished she'd taken a photograph so she could remember exactly what he looked like. Could his eyes really have been as dark as she remembered? She thought about the one real kiss they'd shared and her heart cried out for more.

Several times she found herself in tears. She decided that despite all her own warnings to herself, she was now nursing a broken heart. Eventually, she was forced to confide in her friend, Michelle.

'I knew there was something,' she exclaimed. 'You just haven't been yourself since you came back. Now, come on, spill the beans.'

'There's nothing much to tell.'

'Except you've fallen hook, line and sinker for him, haven't you?'

'I guess. But I knew all along that it could come to nothing. I kept telling myself not to get involved. He promised to get in touch, but I haven't heard a thing. Not a text message. Nothing.'

'He does have your number, I suppose.'

'Course. He promised me a contract with his stores, but I guess the reality of his normal life cut in and he simply forgot.'

Michelle had brought a bottle of wine round and as they drank it, Emily told her much more than she'd intended, including the awful visit from Jemima and the calls from Adam's father. Her friend's advice was to try and forget all about the whole incident.

'However tempting the thought of all his lovely lolly, you don't want that sort of person in your life. You're far too nice for him. He doesn't deserve someone like you.'

'I know you're right, but . . . well, you don't know him.'

'I know the type. Right, Miss Emily Tranter, you and I are going shopping. We're going to get you out of yourself and improve on our social lives from this moment on. Agreed?'

'I don't think so. I'm not sure I can face all that. I need to get over Adam first.'

'Nonsense. We're going to the cinema tomorrow night for a start. There's an excellent film I want to see. Just the thing to cheer you up.'

Emily allowed herself to be persuaded but she found it hard to join in with the banter of the group of friends. She tried to go straight home after the film but they all insisted on her joining them for a drink first. Michelle had said something to the others but without breaking her confidences.

She couldn't wait to get home again and close the door behind herself and the rest of the world. Snickett and Sue seemed to understand that she wasn't her usual self and cuddled close to her whenever they could.

'You're such good friends you two, aren't you?' She was rewarded by two pairs of eyes staring at her and two little tails wagging like tiny windmills. 'You are real friends, undemanding and totally loyal.'

They snuggled closer and she felt tears forming once more. This was ridiculous, she told herself. It was seriously time to get on with her life.

The cheque had arrived for her work, but she needed to look for something to tide her over till the next contract came. She would buy a local paper the next day and see if there were any part-time jobs going and she must forget all about any plans to move to Cornwall. It had been a silly, idealistic plan which would simply never work.

Her mother rang a few days later. She wanted to see Emily and have a talk.

'If it's about Tranter's, Mum, forget it. It was only a bit of a dream.'

'Come over on Sunday. Simon's coming too and we can have a nice Sunday lunch together. Be like old times.'

All right, thanks. But you're not to take it seriously. I know it will spoil all your plans if you don't sell the cottage.'

'Stop worrying. We'll think of something.' She would not be drawn any further and so Emily had to be content to wait. She wondered if her slightly scatty mother would actually remember to buy food for a 'nice Sunday lunch.'

There had been several occasions in the past when they had turned up to find their mother playing tennis, having totally forgotten they'd been invited.

She drove the twenty or so miles to her parents' home and saw Simon's car already parked outside. The dogs were excited to be there again and rushed around greeting everyone.

It was Christmas since they'd all been together and so there was a lot to catch up on. For once, the smell of roasting meat filled the air, so Emily's fears of her mother forgetting they were coming were quite unfounded.

'So, what's this scheme you've been planning?' Emily asked once they'd settled down.

'I'm not sure it will work after all. We've got a valuation on the cottage. Just a rough estimate and it's actually worth a lot more than we expected. Even if you had your share given to you, I doubt you could afford to buy the rest. We were planning to divide it into three and you'd buy us out for the balance. It's only fair that Simon has his share or the equivalent and well, I doubt Dad could afford it, let alone you, still building your careers.'

'But it's nice to know you'd actually consider living in what was my old family home,' her father said. 'Grandad Tranter would have been thrilled.'

'Let Em live there. I can always go and stay whenever. I want, just as I've always done. Shame to let it go out of the family,' Simon suggested.

'Well, yes, but we could all do with

the cash, couldn't we?' Emily insisted.

The conversation went back and forth with ideas being tossed round. The figures made Emily blink at the sheer scale. It was far more than she could ever afford and her thoughts were that it simply was unviable.

'I think you'll have to sell it, Dad. There's no other solution. You're talking about such a lot of money. It would make life so much easier for you and well, it's just a silly idea I had. I would like to go down at least once more though. There's a lot of stuff there that I'd hate to leave behind. Now, how's that roast lamb coming along? It smells wonderful.'

The subject of the Cornish cottage was dropped and they tried to get on to safer topics. Feeling sad, Emily went back to her flat and tried to come to terms with the fact that their beloved cottage would be gone from the family forever. She refused to mope around and planned her attack on the job market for the next day.

She also decided that she should consider the idea of an exhibition. She had already assembled a large portfolio of work and mounting and framing it would be expensive but it was certainly a possibility. It was also a positive thing to be getting on with.

★　★　★

After several days of what seemed like drifting, she began to draw again. Unable to get him out of her mind, she sketched Adam's face, just as she remembered it. There were no details missing. But it still hurt and she pushed the picture away at the bottom of her case. All the same, it felt good to be using her talent properly.

She sketched a series of animals again, subconsciously remembering Adam's suggestion of an Easter theme. She had no idea of what she was working towards but the pleasure of creating something allowed to submerge her thoughts.

She went for several hours without feeling a sense of loss and congratulated herself on getting over him. She was working well when the doorbell rang. The dogs bounded to the door, barking furiously. Their tails were wagging, so she thought they must recognise her caller.

'Hello, Emily. May I come in?'

She gasped as she saw Adam, half hidden by the largest bunch of flowers she had ever seen. She held the door open, unable to speak. Snickett and Sue leapt up to him and were obviously delighted to see him. Sue ran off to find a favourite toy to show him and bounced back, woofing for a game.

'Well, look at you two. You haven't forgotten me, have you? I think your mistress seems to have forgotten me, though. These are for you, by the way.' He handed her the flowers as she stood watching him with her dogs.

'I'm sorry. I'm just amazed to see you. Why didn't you call? I could easily have been out somewhere.'

'I lost your phone number. It's taken me ages to track you down, between working hard. You'd be amazed how many Tranters there are around. I didn't even know if you'd want to see me, let alone where you lived. Just Hertfordshire. Still, I'm here now. Well, aren't I welcome? Do you want me to go away again?'

'Come in. Do you want some coffee?'

'Please. I've had a rather slow drive here and I'm gasping.'

'Thanks for these. They're lovely, but you shouldn't have gone to such expense. How's the leg?'

'It's fine. Not up to playing squash yet, but it's mending well. Dad insisted on a specialist and I've been having physio. So, how are you getting on? Working, I see.'

'Nothing much. I'm toying with the idea of an exhibition. Not that I do that sort of stuff really.'

'So, would you still be interested in the contract I mentioned to you? For the stores?'

'Course I would. Very interested but I thought you'd forgotten or your father scotched the idea. I'll put some coffee on.'

'Emily . . . sit down, please. Stop rushing around like a scalded kitten. Come here, sit by me. I've got a lot to say to you.'

She sat close to him.

'Right. Please listen for a moment. After I got back, I had to listen to several ear bashings from my father. He was very rude about where I'd been and made all sorts of insinuations, mostly fed to him by Jemima, as we thought she might. I tried to tell him that she was jealous but he wouldn't listen. I decided that working with her under those circumstances was no longer tolerable, so I resigned. Much to her delight, of course.'

'But surely not. You can't have left the firm?'

'Oh, but I did. Just for a week. I nearly came to find you there and then but I thought it wouldn't be fair when emotions were running so deep. Once he realised the implications, my father came to see me. I was reinstated and though he still employs the woman, she will no longer be working for the part of the company I'm concerned with. He said that he could never replace me and nor would he want to. Flattering and nice to hear but it was still all a bit of a shock.

'It was while I was unemployed for the week and had some time. I got to thinking seriously about us. I realised that for the first time in my life, I couldn't stop thinking about another person. You were never out of my thoughts. I know that I love you, Emily. I'm sorry it took me so long to tell you. Can you ever forgive me for my awful behaviour and for not getting in touch?'

She sat staring at this man. How ever could she have thought she couldn't remember his beautiful face? His dark eyes? Her portrait wasn't too far out, she thought.

'Well, say something. Do you want

me to leave? Could you ever have feelings for me?'

'Oh, Adam, you must know how I feel. I loved you from the very beginning, despite myself and my good intentions.'

'Even when I was bossy?'

'Maybe. Maybe a bit less then. I thought you didn't care. When you didn't call me . . . '

'Why didn't you call me?'

'I never took your number.'

'But you knew where I work. You could have called if you'd really wanted to.'

'As if I'd make that sort of fool of myself. I assumed you didn't want to know.'

'What a pair of idiots. But, it's all right now, isn't it?'

Shyly, she pulled out the sketch she had made of him.

'I was thinking of you, too.'

'Wow, that's brilliant. A little flattering maybe.'

They talked for a long time, sharing

details of the time since they parted. True to his word, he'd brought a contract with him for designs for the stores. The sum offered was staggering to her and she couldn't wait to sign and get started.

'So, did you decide if you were going to move to Cornwall permanently?'

'Can't afford it. Sadly, the cottage is going to be sold. But, we move on.'

'Do I get to meet your parents?' he asked.

'If you want to.'

'Well, I do feel it's important to meet my future in-laws.' Emily's eyes shone with happiness.

'Is that some sort of proposal?'

'Oh, didn't I say?'

'You know you didn't.'

He fumbled in his pocket and produced a jewellery box.

'You were confident.'

'Not really, but I do like to be prepared. Just in case you said 'yes'. I hope you like it. I thought you'd prefer something simple.' He opened the box

161

to show her the exquisite solitaire diamond. 'If it's the wrong size, it can easily be altered.' He slipped it on to her finger, a perfect fit.

'It's gorgeous. Thank you so much.'

'I can now stand quite unaided so I think it's time to claim that proper kiss.'

He did so.

9

The next few weeks passed in a whirl. Emily's parents were quite shocked at the speed with which things were happening. They both immediately liked Adam and had no objections to them being engaged. They were less certain about a June wedding, however.

'Don't you think you should wait a while? Get to know each other better?'

'Don't really see why. We're both so sure of each other that there's little point waiting.'

'Well, organising a wedding on the scale his family will expect, will take some doing. I mean you have to book a venue in advance and well, it all costs a fortune.'

'Mum, I wouldn't expect you to foot the bill. Besides, Adam's father has offered the use of his house. Marquee in the garden, all that sort of stuff, so I shouldn't worry.'

'Well, I do worry. We do have pride you know.'

After the phone call to her parents, Emily felt worried. Adam had convinced her not to consider the cost of the wedding and she had accepted without too much thought. If her parents wanted to pay, it was a whole new situation. Somehow, she knew that Adam's father would never settle for anything less than a big show.

Once she had met him, she realised what Adam had meant about not arguing and him always being 'right'. One accepted what he said. She had been terrified when going to meet him, but he was a lovely man, if somewhat daunting. An older version of Adam and strikingly handsome.

He had made no comments about her being a gold-digger as he could see Adam's love for her was genuine. Jemima tried her best to cause trouble but soon realised it was pointless. Emily had the feeling that the woman was about to talk herself out of a job and out of their lives if she carried on this way.

'How about just a small family wedding?' Emily suggested. 'And then if your father wants a big do for the people from the stores, we could have a sort of party later, to celebrate. That way my parents' pride remains intact and your father gets his way. Besides, I don't think I want a huge wedding and free for all. The day is for us and not dozens of other people we don't really know.'

'Could work, I guess,' Adam agreed. 'I'll put it to Dad and get back to you.'

In the meantime, Emily and her mother spent hours looking at dresses and flowers and a hundred other things that seemed to be vital, whatever sort of wedding they finally decided on.

Several times, Emily considered the possibility of eloping and getting on with their lives without all the fuss. Her friend, Michelle, was over the moon about it all and as chief bridesmaid, felt it her duty to offer advice at every turn. It was all becoming a nightmare and she wondered if her mother had been right to suggest that June was too soon.

At last the desired compromise was reached and a small family wedding was agreed on. This would take place from her parents' home, followed by a reception at a local hotel.

They would then have a party a couple of days later in the marquee at Adam's home. Emily was dreading the huge gathering that was being planned, but as she was to have her own way for the wedding itself, she accepted that it would be part of her new life.

'This time next week, you'll be Mrs Bryant,' Adam said softly as they finished dinner in a lovely riverside restaurant near his flat. 'We have to decide where we want to live. I know staying at the flat is all right for now, but we need a proper place of our own as soon as possible. I got some details from the local estate agents. Maybe you can give them a look in the morning, before you leave?'

'I can't believe all this is really happening. You are sure about everything, aren't you?'

'Of course. I've never been more sure of anything. And never happier. What about you and all your fears of not fitting in?'

'Maybe I still have moments of doubt . . . not about you of course, but it seems very strange not to have to juggle money all the time. To think, I was planning to try and raise the cash to buy out my parents for the cottage. Now, it's going to be sold anyway.'

'Pity, but I guess one has to be realistic.'

'Easy to say, but it's been a part of my family all my life.'

'I know love. But we have a whole new life ahead of us.'

When she saw the details of the houses Adam had selected, she gasped in amazement. How could anyone afford to pay this much she wondered? In some sort of dream, she flicked through the details.

It made the Cornish cottage she loved so much, seem like a garden shed in comparison.

Her old fears of being unable to cope suddenly rose in her mind. She was out of her depth.

'Adam,' she said in low voice. 'Adam, I still wonder if you aren't making a huge mistake. This isn't me. I could never be happy with a home of this size.' She tossed down the estate agent's details and stood by the window.

'OK, love. We'll wait until you see something you do like.'

'I mean this whole thing. I'm not sure I can go through with it.'

'Em, darling. You know how I feel about you. You can't let me down. Not now.'

'I'm sorry, Adam. It's all too much. Mum was right. We were in too much of a hurry. I'm sorry.' She ran out of the flat, grabbing her bag and keys on the way.

She drove away, tears filling her eyes.

She had no idea where she was going and drove and drove until the car ran out of petrol. Sitting at the roadside, she sobbed, her head resting on the steering wheel. A car stopped beside her and a woman got out.

'Is there something wrong, dear?' she asked kindly.

'I ran out of petrol,' Emily sobbed.

'So, there's no need to cry. I'll give you a lift to the next garage. It isn't far and they'll lend you a can.'

'That's very kind of you. But it isn't the petrol. You see, I've just run away from the most wonderful man in the world. We were getting married next week and I've run away. Left him.'

'Can I ask why? Get in. You can tell me all about it while we drive to the garage.'

'I'm sorry. You don't want to hear all this. Thanks for being so kind.'

'Come on. I'm bursting with curiosity. If he's so wonderful, why have you decided not to marry him?'

'His family are too rich. They don't

realise how the rest of us have to live. I can't deal with all that money.'

'What a nice fault to have. It's usually the other way around. Too little money causes strife. Well, here we are. You must let me know what happens.' The woman thrust a card at her as she got out of the car at the garage. 'Hang on, I'll run you back. I don't like to think of you walking around in this state.'

'I'll be fine,' sobbed Emily. 'Really. You've been more than kind. I suppose it's just wedding nerves.'

Once she got back to the car and put petrol in, she pulled herself together. How could she have cried all over some stranger? She switched on her mobile phone. There were strings of messages, mostly from Adam. She dialled his number.

'I'm sorry. Put it down to nerves.'

'You will be there on Friday, won't you?'

'Course I will. If you still want me to be.'

'Oh Emily. I love you.'

She drove back to her flat. Everything was packed up in boxes, ready to be moved to the flat or to store in Adam's family home. Her flat had been snapped up the first day it was on the market and she was due to vacate it the following day.

It seemed bleak and empty without the dogs, who were already staying with her parents. She was also to stay with them till the wedding day. It seemed that everything in her life was changing at once and she felt the uncertainty hit her once again.

'Michelle? Are you doing anything? Come and share a bottle of wine with me and try to convince me I'm doing the right thing.'

'What?' yelled her friend down the phone. 'What are you talking about? I'll be there in five minutes. If you have any doubts, I'll marry him myself. Adam is the best thing on two legs I've ever seen. Gorgeous looking. Lovely man. And rich with it.'

'That's the problem. He's too rich,'

she moaned, when they'd each had a large glass of wine.

'You're suffering wedding nerves, that's all.'

They talked late into the night and by the time Michelle was leaving, Emily felt better. Nerves was something she'd never experienced before, but she was finally convinced that her friend was right. Once she was with her parents, she felt better. The week passed more happily than they'd all expected and all too soon it was Friday and her wedding day. The phone rang during the morning.

'Guess what? We've had an offer for the cottage. The full asking price. Isn't that a lovely start to the day?'

'I suppose,' Emily agreed, but rather sadly. 'Who's made the offer?'

'Someone wanting a second home. I'd rather it was a local, but well, we can't argue.'

★ ★ ★

It wasn't a typically warm day for June, but once everyone was in church, the ceremony was everything she could have wanted. There was certainly an expression of great relief on Adam's face when she reached him.

'I was so afraid you might leave me waiting here,' he whispered. 'After last Sunday, well . . . '

'I'm sorry. I love you.'

The vicar coughed and everyone stood for the service to begin. Snickett and Sue were waiting outside the church with a friend, white satin bows, badly chewed, hanging vaguely round their necks. Adam bent to stroke them.

'We're all part of the family now girls,' he said as their tails wagged.

The day passed in a sort of dream and all too soon it was over. Her ivory satin dress hung over the wardrobe in their bedroom and she touched it.

'It's such a lovely dress. I can't believe I'll never wear it again.'

'You can wear it if you want to any

time. Especially useful for cookery lessons.'

'Idiot.'

'I've got something for you. A wedding present.'

'You don't have to give me more presents.'

'I know. But I think you might be particularly pleased with this one.' He handed her a large envelope.

'What's this?'

'Open it.'

There were some estate agent details. She looked at him.

'I thought we were going to decide where to live later?' He said nothing and nodded towards the sheaf of papers. She stared. It was a picture of the cottage in Cornwall. Across the picture, it said SOLD in large red letters.

'It's yours. I had my offer accepted this morning. I thought we could go there for our honeymoon. I said it was a surprise . . . I hope it is. We can drive down after the party in a couple of